THE THIEF OF ALWAYS

One of horror master and international bestselling author Clive Barker's classic early novels—the tale of a haunted house with many a dark secret.

Mr. Hood's Holiday House has stood for a thousand years, welcoming children into its embrace. It is a place of miracles where every whim may be satisfied. There is a price to be paid, of course, but young Harvey Swick, bored with his life and beguiled by Mr. Hood's wonders, does not consider the consequences. It is only when the house shows its darker face—when Harvey discovers the pitiful creatures that dwell in its shadows—that he comes to doubt Mr. Hood's generosity.

But the house and its mysterious architect will not release Harvey without a battle. Mr. Hood has plans for his young guest, a boy whose soul burns brighter than any he has encountered in ten centuries. . . .

HARPER PERENNIAL OLIVE EDITIONS

This book is part of a special series from Harper Perennial called Olive Editions—exclusive small-format editions of some of our bestselling and celebrated titles. All Olive Editions are available for a limited time only.

T0146000

THE THIEF OF ALWAYS

THE
THIEF
OF
ALWAYS

A Fable

CLIVE BARKER

Illustrated by Clive Barker

OLIVE

EDITIONS

OLIVE

EDITIONS

A hardcover edition of this book was published in 1992 by HarperCollins Publishers.

THE THIEF OF ALWAYS. Copyright © 1992 by Clive Barker. All rights reserved. Printed in the United States of America. No part of this book may be used or reproduced in any manner whatsoever without written permission except in the case of brief quotations embodied in critical articles and reviews. For information, address HarperCollins Publishers, 195 Broadway, New York, NY 10007.

HarperCollins books may be purchased for educational, business, or sales promotional use. For information, please email the Special Markets Department at SPsales@harpercollins.com.

FIRST HARPER PERENNIAL PAPERBACK PUBLISHED 1993, REISSUED 2008.
FIRST HARPER PERENNIAL OLIVE EDITION PUBLISHED 2024.

Library of Congress Cataloging-in-Publication Data

Names: Barker, Clive, 1952- author, illustrator.
Title: The thief of always : a fable / Clive Barker ; illustrated by Clive Barker.
Description: Harper Perennial Olive edition. | New York : HarperCollins Publishers, 2024.
Identifiers: LCCN 2024005759 | ISBN 9780063413054 (trade paperback)
Subjects: LCSH: Haunted houses--Fiction. | LCGFT: Horror fiction. | Novels.
Classification: LCC PR6052.A6475 T48 2024 | DDC 823/.914--dc23/eng/20240329
LC record available at https://lccn.loc.gov/2024005759

ISBN 978-0-06-341305-4 (Olive edition)

24 25 26 27 28 LBC 5 4 3 2 1

TO M.S.S.

CONTENTS

THE THIEF OF ALWAYS

I

Harvey, Half-Devoured

THE GREAT GRAY BEAST FEBRUARY HAD EATEN HARvey Swick alive. Here he was, buried in the belly of that smothering month, wondering if he would ever find his way out through the cold coils that lay between here and Easter.

He didn't think much of his chances. More than likely he'd become so bored as the hours crawled by that one day he'd simply forget to breathe. Then maybe people would get to wondering why such a fine young lad had perished in his prime. It would become a celebrated mystery, which wouldn't be solved until some great detective decided to re-create a day in Harvey's life.

Then, and only then, would the grim truth be discovered. The detective would first follow Harvey's route to school every morning, trekking through the dismal streets. Then he'd sit at Harvey's desk, and listen to the pitiful drone of the history teacher and the science teacher, and wonder how the heroic boy had managed to keep his eyes open. And finally, as the wasted day dwindled to dusk, he'd trace the homeward trek, and as he set foot on the step from which he had departed that morning, and people asked him—as they would—why such a sweet soul as Harvey had died, he would shake his head and say: "It's very simple."

"Oh?" the curious crowd would say. "Do tell."

And, brushing away a tear, the detective would reply: "Harvey Swick was eaten by the great gray beast February."

IT WAS A MONSTROUS MONTH, THAT WAS FOR SURE; A dire and dreary month. The pleasures of Christmas, both sharp and sweet, were already dimming in Harvey's memory, and the promise of summer was so remote as to be mythical. There'd be a spring break, of course, but how far off was that? Five weeks? Six? Mathematics wasn't his strong point, so he didn't irritate himself further by attempting—and failing—to calculate the days. He simply knew that long before the sun came to save him he would have withered away in the belly of the beast.

"YOU SHOULDN'T WASTE YOUR TIME SITTING UP HERE," HIS mom said when she came in and found him watching the raindrops chase each other down the glass of his bedroom window.

"I've got nothing better to do," Harvey said, without looking around.

"Well then, you can make yourself useful," his mom said.

Harvey shuddered. Useful? That was another word for hard labor. He sprang up, marshaling his excuses—he hadn't done *this*; he hadn't done *that*—but it was too late.

"You can start by tidying up this room," his mom said.

"But—"

"Don't sit wishing the days away, honey. Life's too short."

"But—"

"That's a good boy."

And with that she left him to it. Muttering to himself, he stared around the room. It wasn't even untidy. There were one or two games scattered around; a couple of drawers open; a few clothes hanging out: It looked just fine.

"I am *ten*," he said to himself (having no brothers and sisters, he talked to himself a good deal). "I mean, it's not like I'm a kid. I don't have to tidy up just because *she* says so. It's boring."

He wasn't just muttering now, he was talking out loud.

"I want to . . . I want to . . ." He went to the mirror, and quizzed it. "What *do* I want?" The straw-haired, snub-nosed, brown-eyed boy he saw before him shook his head. "I don't know what I want," he said. "I just know I'll die if I don't have some fun. I will! I'll die!"

As he spoke, the window rattled. A gust of wind blew hard against it—then a second; then a third—and even though Harvey didn't remember the window being so much as an inch ajar, it was suddenly thrown open. Cold rain spattered his face. Half-closing his eyes, he crossed to the window and fumbled to slam it, making sure that the latch was in place this time.

The wind had started his lamp moving, and when he turned back the whole room seemed to be swinging around. One moment the light was blazing in his eyes, the next it was flooding the opposite wall. But in between the blaze and the flood it lit the middle of his room, and standing there—shaking the rain off his hat—was a stranger.

He looked harmless enough. He was no more than six inches taller than Harvey, his frame scrawny, his skin distinctly yellowish in color. He was wearing a fancy suit, a pair of spectacles and a lavish smile.

"Who are you?" Harvey demanded, wondering how he could get past this interloper to the door.

"Don't be nervous," the man replied, teasing off one of his suede gloves, taking Harvey's hand and shaking it. "My name's Rictus. You *are* Harvey Swick, aren't you?"

"Yes . . ."

"I thought for a moment I'd got the wrong house."

Harvey couldn't take his eyes off Rictus's grin. It was wide enough to shame a shark, with two perfect rows of gleaming teeth.

Rictus took off his spectacles, pulled a handkerchief from the pocket of his waterlogged jacket, then started to mop off the raindrops. Either he or the handkerchief gave off an odor that was far from fragrant. The smell, in truth, was flatulent.

"You've got questions, I can see that," Rictus said to Harvey.

"Yeah."

"Ask away. I've got nothing to hide."

"Well, how did you get in, for one thing?"

"Through the window, of course."

"It's a long way up from the street."

"Not if you're flying."

"Flying?"

"Of course. How else was I going to get around on a foul night like this? It was either that or a rowboat. We short folk gotta watch out when it's raining this hard. One wrong step and you're swimming." He peered at Harvey quizzically. "Do you swim?"

"In the summer, sometimes," Harvey replied, wanting to get back to the business of flying.

But Rictus took the conversation in another direction entirely. "On nights like this," he said, "doesn't it seem like there'll never *be* another summer?"

"It sure does," said Harvey.

"You know I heard you sighing a mile off, and I said to myself: '*There's* a kid who needs a vacation.'" He consulted his watch. "If you've got the time, that is."

"The time?"

"For a trip, boy, for a trip! You need an adventure, young Swick. Somewhere . . . *out of this world.*"

"How'd you hear me sighing when you were a mile away?" Harvey wanted to know.

"Why should you care? I heard you. That's all that matters."

"Is it magic of some kind?"

"Maybe."

"Why won't you tell me?"

Rictus gave Harvey a beady stare. "I think you're too inquisitive for your own good, that's why," he said, his smile decaying a little. "If you don't *want* help, that's fine by me."

He made a move toward the window. The wind was still

gusting against the glass, as though eager to come back in and carry its passenger away.

"*Wait,*" Harvey said.

"For what?"

"I'm sorry. I won't ask any more questions."

Rictus halted, his hand on the latch. "No more questions, eh?"

"I promise," said Harvey. "I told you: I'm sorry."

"So you did. So you did." Rictus peered out at the rain. "I know a place where the days are always sunny," he said, "and the nights are full of wonders."

"Could you take me there?"

"We said no questions, boy. We agreed."

"Oh. Yeah. I'm sorry."

"Being a forgiving sort, I'll forget you spoke, and I'll tell you this: If you want me to inquire on your behalf, I'll see if they've got room for another guest."

"I'd like that."

"I'm not guaranteeing anything," Rictus said, opening the latch.

"I understand."

The wind gusted suddenly, and blew the window wide. The light began to swing wildly.

"Watch for me," Rictus yelled above the din of rain and wind.

Harvey started to ask him if he'd be coming back soon, but stopped himself in the nick of time.

"*No questions, boy!*" Rictus said, and as he spoke the wind seemed to fill up his coat. It rose around him like a black balloon, and he was suddenly swept out over the windowsill.

"*Questions rot the mind!*" he hollered as he went. "*Keep your mouth shut and we'll see what comes your way!*"

And with that the wind carried him off, the balloon of his coat rising like a black moon against the rainy sky.

II

The Hidden Way

Harvey said nothing about his peculiar visitor to either his mom or his dad, in case they put locks on the windows to stop Rictus returning to the house. But the trouble with keeping the visit a secret was that after a few days Harvey began to wonder if he'd imagined the whole thing. Perhaps he'd fallen asleep at the window, he thought, and Rictus had simply been a dream.

He kept hoping nevertheless. "Watch for me," Rictus had said, and Harvey did just that. He watched from the window of his room. He watched from his desk at school. He even watched with one eye when he was lying on his pillow at night. But Rictus didn't show.

And then, about a week after that first visit, just as Harvey's hope was waning, his watchfulness was rewarded. On his way to school one foggy morning he heard a voice above his head, and looked up to see Rictus floating down from the clouds, his coat swelled up around him so that he looked fatter than a prize pig.

"Howya doin'?" he said, as he descended.

"I was starting to think I'd invented you," Harvey replied. "You know, like a dream."

"I get that a lot," Rictus said, his smile wider than ever. "Particularly from the ladies. You're a dream come true, they say." He winked. "And who am I to argue? You like my shoes?"

Harvey looked down at Rictus's bright blue shoes. They were quite a sight, and he said so.

"I got given 'em by my boss," Rictus said. "He's very happy you're going to come visit. So, are you ready?"

"Well . . ."

"It's no use wasting time," Rictus said. "There may not be room for you tomorrow."

"Can I just ask *one* question?"

"I thought we agreed—"

"I know. But just one."

"All right. One."

"Is this place far from here?"

"Nah. It's just across town."

"So I'd only be missing a couple of hours of school?"

"That's two questions," Rictus said.

"No, I'm just thinking out loud."

Rictus grunted. "Look," he said, "I'm not here to do a great song and dance persuading you. I got a friend called Jive does that. I'm just a smiler. I smile, and I say: Come with me to the Holiday House, and if folks don't want to come—" He shrugged. "Hey, it's their hard luck."

With that, he turned his back on Harvey.

"Wait!" Harvey protested. "I want to come. But just for a little while."

"You can stay as long as you like," Rictus said. "Or as little. All I want to do is take that glum expression off your face and put one of *these* up there." His grin grew even larger. "Is there any crime in that?"

"No," said Harvey. "That's no crime. I'm glad you found me. I really am."

So what if he missed *all* of the morning at school, he thought, it'd be no great loss. Maybe an hour or two of the afternoon as well. As long as he was back home by three. Or four. Certainly before dark.

"I'm ready to go," he said to Rictus. "Lead the way."

MILLSAP, THE TOWN IN WHICH HARVEY HAD LIVED ALL his life, wasn't very big, and he thought he'd seen just about all of it over the years. But the streets he knew were soon behind them, and though Rictus was setting a fair speed Harvey made sure he kept a mental list of landmarks along the way, in case he had to find his way home on his own. A butcher's shop with two pigs' heads hanging from hooks; a church with a yard full of old tombs beside it; the statue of some dead general, covered from hat to stirrups in pigeon dung: All these sights and more he noted and filed away.

And while they walked, Rictus kept up a stream of idle chatter.

"I hate the fog! Just hate it!" he said. "And there'll be rain by noon. We'll be out of it, of course..." He went on from talk of rain to the state of the streets. "Look at this trash, all over the sidewalk! It's shameful! And the mud! It's making a fine old mess of my shoes!"

He had plenty more to say, but none of it was very enlightening, so after a while Harvey gave up listening. How far *was* this Holiday House, he began to wonder. The fog was chilling him, and his legs were aching. If they didn't get there soon, he was going to turn back.

"I know what you're thinking," said Rictus.

"I bet you don't."

"You're thinking this is all a trick. You're thinking Rictus is leading you on a mystery tour and there's nothing at the end of it. Isn't that true?"

"Maybe a little."

"Well, my boy, I've got news for you. Look up ahead."

He pointed, and there—not very far from where they stood—was a high wall, which was so long that it disappeared into the fog to right and left.

"What do you see?" Rictus asked him.

"A wall," Harvey replied, though the more he stared at it the less certain of this he was. The stones, which had seemed solid enough at first sight, now looked to be shifting and wavering, as though they'd been chiseled from the fog itself, and piled up here to keep out prying eyes.

"It *looks* like a wall," Harvey said, "but it's *not* a wall."

"You're very observant," Rictus replied admiringly. "Most people just see a dead end, so they turn around and take another street."

"But not us."

"No, not us. We're going to keep on walking. You know why?"

"Because the Holiday House is on the other side?"

"What a *mir-ac-u-lous* kid you are!" Rictus replied. "That's exactly right. Are you hungry, by the way?"

"Starving."

"Well, there's a woman waiting for you in the House called Mrs. Griffin, and let me tell you, she is the greatest cook in all of Americaland. I swear, on my tailor's grave. Anything you can dream of eating, she can cook. All you have to do is ask. Her deviled eggs—" He smacked his lips. "Perfection."

"I don't see a gate," Harvey said.

"That's because there isn't one."

"So how do we get in?"

"Just keep walking!"

Half out of hunger, half out of curiosity, Harvey did as Rictus had instructed, and as he came within three steps of the wall a gust of balmy, flower-scented wind slipped between the shimmering stones and kissed his cheek. Its warmth was welcome after his long, cold trek, and he picked up his pace, reaching out to touch the wall as he approached it. The misty stones seemed to reach for him in their turn, wrapping their soft, gray arms around his shoulders, and ushering him through the wall.

He looked back, but the street he'd stepped out of, with its gray sidewalks and gray clouds, had already disappeared. Beneath his feet the grass was high and full of flowers. Above his head, the sky was mid-summer blue. And ahead of him, set at the summit of a great slope, was a house that had surely been first imagined in a dream.

He didn't wait to see if Rictus was coming after him, nor to wonder how the gray beast February had been slain and this warm day risen in its place. He simply let out a laugh that Rictus would have been proud of, and hurried up the slope and into the shadow of the dream house.

III

Pleasure and the Worm

WHAT A FINE THING IT WOULD BE, HARVEY THOUGHT, to build a place like this. To drive its foundations deep into the earth; to lay its floors and hoist its walls; to say: Where there was nothing, I raised a house. That would be a very fine thing.

It wasn't a puffed-up peacock of a place, either. There were no marble steps, no fluted columns. It was a proud house, certainly, but there was nothing wrong with that; it had much to be proud *of*. It stood four stories high, and boasted more windows than Harvey could readily count. Its porch was wide, as were the steps that led up to its carved front door; its slated roofs were steep and crowned with magnificent chimneys and lightning rods.

Its highest point, however, was neither a chimney nor a lightning rod, but a large and elaborately wrought weathervane, which Harvey was peering up at when he heard the front door open and a voice say:

"Harvey Swick, as I live and breathe."

He looked down, the weathervane's white silhouette still behind his eyes, and there on the porch stood a woman who made his grandmother (the oldest person he knew) look young. She had a face like a rolled-up ball of cobwebs, from which her hair, which could also have been spiders' work, fell in wispy abundance. Her eyes were tiny, her mouth tight, her hands gnarled. Her voice, however, was melodious, and its words welcoming.

"I thought maybe you'd decided not to come," she said, picking up a basket of freshly cut flowers she'd left on the step, "which would have been a pity. Come on in! There's food on the table. You must be famished."

"I can't stay long," Harvey said.

"You must do whatever you wish," came the reply. "I'm Mrs. Griffin, by the way."

"Yes, Rictus mentioned you."

"I hope he didn't bend your ear too much. He loves the sound of his own voice. That and his reflection."

Harvey had climbed the porch steps by now, and stopped in front of the open door. This was a moment of decision, he knew, though he wasn't quite certain why.

"Step inside," Mrs. Griffin said, brushing a spider-hair back from her furrowed brow.

But Harvey still hesitated, and he might have turned around and never stepped inside the House except that he heard a boy's voice yelling:

"I got ya! I got ya!" followed by uproarious laughter.

"Wendell!" Mrs. Griffin said. "Are you chasing the cats again?"

The sound of laughter grew even louder, and it was so full of good humor that Harvey stepped over the threshold and into the House just so that he could see the face of its owner.

He only got a brief look. A goofy, bespectacled face appeared for a moment at the other end of the hallway. Then a piebald cat dashed between the boy's legs and he was off after it, yelling and laughing again.

"He's such a crazy boy," Mrs. Griffin said, "but all the cats love him!"

The House was more wonderful inside than out. Even on the short journey to the kitchen Harvey glimpsed enough to know that this was a place built for games, chases and adventures. It was a maze in which no two doors were alike. It was a treasure-house where some notorious pirate had hidden his blood-stained booty. It was a resting place for carpets flown by *djinns,* and boxes sealed before the Flood, where the eggs of beasts that the earth had lost were wrapped and waiting for the sun's heat to hatch them.

"It's perfect!" Harvey murmured to himself.

Mrs. Griffin caught his words. "Nothing's perfect," she replied.

"Why not?"

"Because time passes," she went on, staring down at the flowers she'd cut. "And the beetle and the worm find their way into everything sooner or later."

Hearing this, Harvey wondered what grief it was Mrs. Griffin had known or seen to make her so mournful.

"I'm sorry," she said, covering her melancholy with a tiny smile. "You didn't come here to listen to my dirges. You came to enjoy yourself, didn't you?"

"I guess I did," Harvey said.

"So let me tempt you with some treats."

Harvey sat himself down at the kitchen table, and within sixty seconds Mrs. Griffin had set a dozen plates of food in front of him: hamburgers, hot dogs and fried chicken; mounds of buttered potatoes; apple, cherry and mud pies, ice cream and whipped cream; grapes, tangerines and a plate of fruits he couldn't even name.

He set to eating with gusto, and was devouring his second slice of pie when a freckled girl with long, frizzy blond hair and huge, blue-green eyes ambled in.

"You must be Harvey," she said.

"How did you know?"

"Wendell told me."

"How did *he* know?"

She shrugged. "He just heard. I'm Lulu, by the way."

"Did you just arrive?"

"No. I've been here for ages. Longer than Wendell. But not as long as Mrs. Griffin. Nobody's been here as long as she has. Isn't that right?"

"Almost," said Mrs. Griffin, a little mysteriously. "Do you want something to eat, sweetie?"

Lulu shook her head. "No thanks. I haven't got much of an appetite at the moment."

She nevertheless sat down opposite Harvey, stuck her thumb in the mud pie, and licked it clean.

"Who invited you here?" she asked.

"A guy called Rictus."

"Oh yeah. The one with the grin?"

"That's him."

"He's got a sister and two brothers," she went on.

"You've met them then?"

"Not all of them," Lulu admitted. "They keep themselves to themselves. But you'll meet one or two of them sooner or later."

"I . . . don't think I'll be staying," Harvey said. "I mean my mom and dad don't even know I'm here."

"Sure they do," Lulu replied. "They just didn't tell you about it." This confused Harvey, and he said so. "Call your mom and dad," Lulu suggested. "Ask 'em."

"Can I do that?" he wondered.

"Of course you can," Mrs. Griffin replied. "The phone's in the hallway."

Carrying a spoonful of ice cream with him, Harvey went to the phone and dialled. At first there was a whining sound on the line, as though a wind were in the wires. Then, as it cleared, he heard his mom say: "Who is this?"

"Before you start yelling—" he began.

"Oh, honey," his mom cooed. "Did you arrive?"

"Arrive?"

"You *are* at the Holiday House, I hope."

"Yes, I am. But—"

"Oh, good. I was worried maybe you'd lost your way. Do you like it there?"

"You knew I was coming?" Harvey said, catching Lulu's eye.

I told you, she mouthed.

"Of *course* we knew," his mom went on. "We invited Mr. Rictus to show you the place. You looked so sad, you poor lamb. We thought you needed a little fun."

"Really?" said Harvey, astonished by this turn of events.

"We just want you to enjoy yourself," his mom went on. "So you stay just as long as you want."

"What about school?" he said.

"You deserve a little time off," came the reply. "Don't you worry about anything. Just have a good time."

"I will, Mom."

"'Bye, honey."

"'Bye."

Harvey came away from the conversation shaking his head in amazement.

"You were right," he said to Lulu. "They arranged everything."

"So now you don't have to feel guilty," said Lulu. "Well, I guess I'll see you around later, huh?"

And with that she ambled away.

"If you're finished eating," Mrs. Griffin said, "I'll show you to your room."

"I'd like that."

She duly led Harvey up the stairs. At the landing, basking on the sun-drenched windowsill, was a cat with fur the color of the cloudless sky.

"That's Blue-Cat," Mrs. Griffin said. "You saw Stew-Cat playing with Wendell. I don't know where Clue-Cat is, but he'll find you. He likes new guests."

"Do you have a lot of people coming here?"

"Only children. Very special children like you and Lulu and Wendell. Mr. Hood won't have just anybody."

"Who's Mr. Hood?"

"The man who built the Holiday House," Mrs. Griffin replied.

"Will I meet him too?"

Mrs. Griffin looked discomfited by the question. "Maybe," she said, her gaze averted. "But he's a very private man."

They were up on the landing by now, and Mrs. Griffin led Harvey past a row of painted portraits to a room at the back of the House. It overlooked an orchard, and the warm air carried the smell of ripe apples into the room.

"You look tired, my sweet," Mrs. Griffin said. "Maybe you should lie down for a little while."

Harvey usually hated to sleep in the afternoon; it reminded him too much of having the flu, or the measles. But the pillow looked very cool and comfortable, and when Mrs.

Griffin had taken her leave he decided to lie down, just for a few minutes.

Either he was more tired than he'd thought, or the calm and comfort of the House rocked him into a slumber. Whichever, his eyes closed almost as soon as he put his head on the pillow, and they did not open again until morning.

IV

A Death between Seasons

THE SUN CAME TO WAKE HIM SOON AFTER DAWN—A straight white dart of light, laid on his lids. He sat up with a start, wondering for a moment what bed this was, what room, what house. Then his memories of the previous day returned, and he realized that he'd slept through from late afternoon to early morning. The rest had strengthened him. He felt energetic, and with a whoop of pleasure he jumped out of bed and got dressed.

The House was more welcoming than ever today, the flowers Mrs. Griffin had set on every table and sill singing with color. The front door stood open, and sliding down the gleaming banisters Harvey raced out onto the porch to inspect the morning.

A surprise awaited him. The trees which had been heavy with leaves the previous afternoon had shed their canopies. There were new, tiny buds on every branch and twig, as though this were the first day of spring.

"Another day, another dollar," said Wendell, ambling around the corner of the House.

"What does that mean?" said Harvey.

"It's what my father used to say all the time. *Another day, another dollar.* He's a banker, my dad. Wendell Hamilton the Second. And me, I'm—"

"Wendell Hamilton the Third."

"How'd ya know?"

"Lucky guess. I'm Harvey."

"Yeah, I know. D'ya like tree houses?"

"I never had one."

Wendell pointed up at the tallest tree. There was a platform perched up among the branches, with a rudimentary house built upon it.

"I've been working up there for weeks," said Wendell, "but I can't get it finished alone. Ya want to help me?"

"Sure. But I've got to eat something first."

"Go eat. I'll be around."

Harvey headed back inside, and found Mrs. Griffin setting out a breakfast fit for a prince. There was milk spilt on the floor, and a cat with a tail hooked like a question mark lapping it up.

"Clue-Cat?" he said.

"Yes indeed," Mrs. Griffin said fondly. "He's the wicked one."

Clue-Cat looked up, as if he knew he was being talked about. Then he jumped up onto the table and searched among the plates of pancakes and waffles for something more to eat.

"Can he do whatever he likes?" Harvey said, watching the cat sniff at this and that. "I mean, does nobody control him?"

"Ah, well, we all have *somebody* watching over us, don't we?" Mrs. Griffin replied. "Whether we like it or not. Now eat. You've got some wonderful times ahead of you."

Harvey didn't need a second invitation. He dug into his second meal at the Holiday House with even more appetite than he had the first, and then headed out to meet the day.

Oh, what a day it was!

The breeze was warm, and smelled of the green scent of growing things; the perfect sky was full of swooping birds. He sauntered through the grass, his hands in his pockets, like the lord of all he surveyed, calling to Wendell as he approached the trees.

"Can I come up?"

"If you've got a head for heights," Wendell dared him.

The ladder creaked as he climbed, but he made the platform without missing a step. Wendell was impressed.

"Not bad for a new boy," he said. "We had two kids here couldn't even get halfway up."

"Where'd they go?"

"Back home, I s'pose. Kids come and go, you know?"

Harvey peered out through the branches, upon which every bud was bursting.

"You can't see much, can you?" he said. "I mean, there's no sign of the town at all."

"Who cares?" said Wendell. "It's just gray out there anyway."

"And it's sunny here," Harvey said, staring down at the wall of misty stones that divided the grounds of the House from the outside world. "How's that possible?"

Wendell's answer was the same again: "Who cares?" he said. "I know *I* don't. Now, are we going to start building, or what?"

THEY SPENT THE NEXT TWO HOURS WORKING ON THE tree house, descending a dozen times to dig through the timbers heaped beside the orchard, looking for boards to finish their repairs. By noon they'd not only found enough wood to fix the roof, but they had each found a friend. Harvey liked Wendell's bad jokes, and that *who cares?* which found its way into every other sentence. And Wendell seemed just as happy to have Harvey's company.

"You're the first kid who's been real fun," he said.

"What about Lulu?"

"What about her?"

"Isn't she any fun?"

"She was okay when I first arrived," Wendell admitted. "I mean, she's been here *months,* so she kinda showed me the place. But she's gotten weird the last few days. I see her sometimes wanderin' around like she's sleepwalkin', with a blank expression on her face."

"She's probably going crazy," Harvey said. "Her brain's turning to mush."

"Do you know about that stuff?" Wendell wanted to know, his face lighting up with ghoulish delight.

"Sure I do," Harvey lied. "My dad's a surgeon."

Wendell was most impressed by this, and for the next few minutes listened in gaping envy as Harvey told him about all the operations he'd seen: skulls sawn open and legs sawn off; feet sewn on where hands used to be, and a man with a boil on his behind that grew into a talking head.

"You swear?" said Wendell.

"I swear," said Harvey.

"That's so cool."

All this talk brought on a fierce hunger, and at Wendell's suggestion they climbed down the ladder and wandered into the House to eat.

"What do you want to do this afternoon?" he asked Harvey as they sat down at the table. "It's going to be real hot. It always is."

"Is there anywhere we can swim?"

Wendell frowned. "Well, yes . . ." he said doubtfully. "There's a lake around the other side of the House, but you won't much like it."

"Why not?"

"The water's so deep you can't even see the bottom."

"Are there any fish?"

"Oh sure."

"Maybe we could catch some. Mrs. Griffin could cook 'em for us."

At this, Mrs. Griffin, who was at the stove piling up a plate with onion rings, gave a little shout, and dropped the plate. She turned to Harvey, her face ashen.

"You don't want to do that," she said.

"Why not?" Harvey replied. "I thought I could do whatever I wanted."

"Well, yes, of course you can," she told him. "But I wouldn't want you to get sick. The fish are . . . poisonous, you see."

"Oh," said Harvey, "well, maybe we won't eat 'em after all."

"Look at this mess," Mrs. Griffin said, fussing to cover her confusion. "I need a new apron."

She hurried away to fetch one, leaving Harvey and Wendell to exchange puzzled looks.

"Now I *really* have to see those fish," Harvey said.

As he spoke, the ever inquisitive Clue-Cat jumped up onto the counter beside the stove, and before either of the boys could move to stop him he had his paws up on the lip of one of the pans.

"Hey, get down!" Harvey told him.

The cat didn't care to take orders. He hoisted himself up onto the rim of the pan to sniff at its contents, his tail flicking back and forth. The next moment, disaster. The tail danced too close to one of the burners and burst into flames. Clue-Cat yowled, and tipped over the pan he was perched upon. A wave of boiling water washed him off the top of the stove, and he fell to the ground in a smoking heap. Whether drowned, scalded or incinerated, the end was the same: He hit the floor dead.

The din brought Mrs. Griffin hurrying back.

"I think I'm going to go eat outside," Wendell said as the old woman appeared at the door. He snatched up a couple hot dogs, and was gone.

"Oh my Lord!" Mrs. Griffin cried when she set eyes on the dead cat. "Oh . . . you foolish thing."

"It was an accident," Harvey said, sickened by what had happened. "He was up on the stove—"

"Foolish thing. Foolish thing," was all Mrs. Griffin seemed able to say. She sank down onto her knees, and stared at the sad little sack of burned fur. "No more questions from you," she finally murmured.

The sight of Mrs. Griffin's unhappiness made Harvey's eyes sting, but he hated to have anyone see him cry, so he fought back his tears as best he could and said: "Shall I help you bury him?" in his gruffest voice.

Mrs. Griffin looked around. "That's very sweet of you," she said softly. "But there's no need. You go out and play."

"I don't want to leave you on your own," Harvey said.

"Oh, look at you, child," Mrs. Griffin said. "You've got tears on your cheeks."

Harvey blushed and wiped them away with the back of his hand.

"Don't be ashamed to weep," Mrs. Griffin said. "It's a wonderful thing. I wish I could still shed a tear or two."

"You're sad," Harvey said. "I can see that."

"What I feel is not quite sadness," Mrs. Griffin replied. "And it's not much solace, either, I'm afraid."

"What's solace?" Harvey asked.

"It's something soothing," Mrs. Griffin said, getting to her feet. "Something that heals the pain in your heart."

"And you don't have any of that?"

"No, I don't," Mrs. Griffin said. She reached out and touched Harvey's cheek. "Except maybe in these tears of yours. They comfort me." She sighed as she traced their tracks with her fingers. "Your tears are sweet, child. And so are you. Now you go out into the light and enjoy yourself. There's sun on the step, and it won't be there forever, believe me."

"Are you sure?"

"I'm sure."

"I'll see you later then," Harvey said, and headed out into the afternoon.

V

The Prisoners

THE TEMPERATURE HAD RISEN WHILE HARVEY HAD been at lunch. A heat-haze hovered over the lawn (which was lusher and more thick with flowers than he remembered) and it made the trees around the House shimmer.

He headed toward them, calling Wendell's name as he went. There was no reply. He glanced back toward the House, thinking he might see Wendell at one of the windows, but they were all reflecting the pristine blue. He looked from House to heavens. There was not a cloud in sight.

And now a suspicion stole upon him, which grew into a certainty as his gaze wandered back to the shimmering copse and the flowers underfoot. During the hour he'd spent in the cool of the kitchen the season had changed. Summer had come to Mr. Hood's Holiday House; a summer as magical as the spring that had preceded it.

That was why the sky was so faultlessly blue, and the birds making such music. The leaf-laden branches were no less content; nor the blossoms in the grass, nor the bees that buzzed from bloom to bloom, gathering the season's bounty. All were in bliss.

It would not be a long season, Harvey guessed. If the spring had been over in a morning, then most likely this perfect summer would not outlast the afternoon.

I'd better make the most of it, he thought, and hurried in search of Wendell. He finally discovered his friend sitting in the shade of the trees, with a pile of comics at his side.

"Wanna sit down and read?" he asked.

"Maybe later," said Harvey. "First I want to go look at this lake you were talking about. Are you going to come?"

"What for? I told you it's no fun."

"All right, I'll go on my own."

"You won't stay long," Wendell remarked, and went back to his reading.

Though Harvey had a good idea of the lake's general whereabouts, the bushes on that side of the House were thick and thorny, and it took him several minutes to find a way through them. By the time he caught sight of the lake itself the sweat on his face and back was clammy, and his arms had been scratched and bloodied by barbs.

As Wendell had predicted, the lake wasn't worth the trouble. It was large—so large that the far side was barely visible—but gloomy and drear, both the lake and the dark stones around it covered with a film of green scum. There was a legion of flies buzzing around in search of something rotten to feed on, and Harvey guessed they'd have no trouble finding a feast. This was a place where dead things belonged.

He was about to leave when a movement in the shadows caught his eye. Somebody was standing further along the bank, almost eclipsed by the mesh of thicket. He moved a few paces closer to the lake, and saw that it was Lulu. She was perched on the slimy stones at the very edge of the water, gazing into their depths.

Speaking in a near whisper for fear he'd startle her, Harvey said:

"It looks cold."

She glanced up at him, her face full of confusion, and then—without a word of reply—turned and bounded away through the bushes.

"Wait!" Harvey called, hurrying toward the lake.

Lulu had already disappeared, however, leaving the thicket

shaking. He might have gone in pursuit of her, but the sound of bubbles breaking in the lake took his gaze to the waters, and there, moving just below the coating of scum, he saw the fish. They were almost as large as he was, their gray scales stained and encrusted, their bulbous eyes turned up toward the surface like the eyes of prisoners in a watery pit.

They were watching him, he was certain of that, and their scrutiny made him shudder. Were they hungry, he wondered, and praying to their fishy gods that he'd slip on the stones and tumble in? Or were they wishing he'd come with a rod and a line, so that they could be hauled from the depths and put out of their misery?

What a life, he thought. No sun to warm them; no flowers to sniff at or games to play. Just the deep, dark waters to circle in; and circle, and circle, and circle.

It made him dizzy just watching, and he feared that if he lingered much longer he'd lose his balance and join them. Gasping with relief he turned his back on the sight, and returned into the sunlight as fast as the barbs would allow.

Wendell was still sitting underneath the tree. He had two bottles of ice-cold soda in the grass beside him, and lobbed one to Harvey as he approached.

"Well?" he said.

"You were right," Harvey replied.

"Nobody in their right minds ever goes there."

"I saw Lulu."

"What did I tell you?" Wendell crowed. "Nobody in their right minds."

"And those fish—"

"Yeah, I know," Wendell said, pulling a face. "Ugly boogers, aren't they?"

"Why would Mr. Hood have fish like that? I mean,

everything else is so beautiful. The lawns, the House, the orchard . . ."

"Who cares?" said Wendell.

"I do," said Harvey. "I want to know everything there is to know about this place."

"Why?"

"So I can tell my mom and dad about it when I go home."

"Home?" said Wendell. "Who needs it? We've got everything we need here."

"I'd still like to know how all this works. Is there some kind of machine making the seasons change?"

Wendell pointed up through the branches at the sun. "Does *that* look mechanical to you?" he said. "Don't be a dope, Harvey. This is all real. It's magic, but it's real."

"You think so?"

"It's too hot to *think,*" Wendell replied. "Now sit down and shut up." He tossed a few comics in Harvey's direction. "Look through these. Find yourself a monster for tonight."

"What's happening tonight?"

"Halloween, of course," Wendell said. "It happens every night."

Harvey plunked himself down beside Wendell, opened his soda, and began to leaf through the comics, thinking as he leafed and sipped that maybe Wendell was right, and it *was* too hot to think. However this miraculous place worked, it seemed real enough. The sun was hot, the soda was cold, the sky was blue, the grass was green. What more did he need to know?

Somewhere in the middle of these musings he must have dozed off, because he woke with a start to find that the sun was no longer dappling the ground around him, and Wendell was no longer reading at his side.

He reached for his soda, but the bottle had fallen over, and the scent of sweet cherry had attracted hundreds of ants.

They were crawling over it and into it, many drowning for their greed.

As he got to his feet the first real breeze he'd felt since noon blew, and a leaf, its edges sere, spiraled down to land at his feet.

"Autumn . . ." he murmured to himself.

Until this moment, standing beneath the creaking boughs watching the wind shake down the leaves, autumn had always seemed to him the saddest of seasons. It meant that summer was over, and the nights would be growing long and cold. But now, as the drizzle of leaves became a deluge, and the patter of acorns and chestnuts a drumming, he laughed to see and hear its coming. By the time he was out from under the trees he had leaves in his hair, and down his back, and was kicking them up with every racing step.

As he reached the porch, the first clouds he'd seen all afternoon crept over the sun, and their shadow made the House, which had wavered in the heat of the afternoon like a mirage, suddenly *loom,* dark and solid.

"You're real," he said, as he stood panting on the porch. "You are, aren't you?"

He started to laugh at the foolishness of talking to a House, but the smile went from his face as a voice, so soft he was barely certain he heard it, said:

"What do you think, child?"

He looked for the speaker, but there was nobody at the threshold, nor out on the porch, nor on the steps behind him.

"Who said that?" he demanded.

There was no answer, which he was glad of. It hadn't been a voice at all, he told himself. It had been a creak of the boards underfoot, or the rustling of dry leaves in the grass. But he stepped into the House with his heart beating a little faster, reminding himself as he went that questions weren't welcome here.

What did it matter, anyway, he thought, whether this was a real place or a dream? It *felt* real, and that was all that mattered.

Satisfied with this, he raced through the House into the kitchen where Mrs. Griffin was weighing the table down with treats.

VI

Seen and Unseen

W ELL," SAID WENDELL AS THEY ATE, "WHAT ARE YOU going to be tonight?"

"I don't know," Harvey said. "What are you going to be?"

"A hangman," he said, with a spaghetti grin. "I've been learning how to tie nooses. Now all I've got to do is find someone to hang." He eyed Mrs. Griffin. "It's quick," he said. "You just drop 'em and—snap!—their necks break!"

"That's horrible!" Mrs. Griffin said. "Why do boys always love talking about ghosts and murders and hangings?"

"Because it's exciting," Wendell said.

"You're monsters," she replied, with a hint of a smile. "That's what you are. Monsters."

"Harvey is," Wendell said. "I've seen him filing down his teeth."

"Is it a full moon?" Harvey said, smearing ketchup around his mouth and putting on a twitch. "I hope so. I need blood . . . *fresh blood.*"

"Good," said Wendell. "You can be a vampire. I'll hang 'em and you can suck their blood."

"Horrible," Mrs. Griffin said again, "just horrible."

Perhaps the House had heard Harvey wishing for a full moon, because when he and Wendell traipsed upstairs and looked out the landing window, there—hanging between the bare branches of the trees—was a moon as wide and as white as a dead man's smile.

"Look at it!" Harvey said. "I can see every crater. It's perfect."

"Oh that's just the start," Wendell promised, and led

Harvey to a large, musty room which had been filled with clothes of every description. Some were hung on hooks and coat hangers. Some were in baskets, like actors' costumes. Still more were heaped at the far end of the room on the dusty floor. And, half-hidden until Wendell cleared the way, was a sight that made Harvey gasp: a wall covered from floor to ceiling with masks.

"Where did they all come from?" Harvey said as he gaped at this spectacle.

"Mr. Hood collects them," Wendell explained. "And the clothes are just stuff that kids who visited here left behind."

Harvey wasn't interested in the clothes, it was the masks that mesmerized him. They were like snowflakes: no two alike. Some were made of wood and of plastic; some of straw and cloth and papier-mâché. Some were as bright as parrots, others as pale as parchment. Some were so grotesque he was certain they'd been carved by crazy people; others so perfect they looked like the death masks of angels. There were masks of clowns and foxes, masks like skulls decorated with real teeth, and one with carved flames instead of hair.

"Take your pick," said Wendell. "There's bound to be a vampire somewhere. Whatever I come in here wanting to find, I find it sooner or later."

Harvey decided to leave the pleasure of choosing a mask until last, and concentrated instead on digging up something suitably batlike to wear. As he worked through the piles of clothes he found himself wondering about the children who'd left them here. Though he'd always hated history lessons, he knew some of the jackets and shoes and shirts and belts had been out of fashion for many, many years. Where were their owners now? Dead, he presumed, or so old it made no difference.

The thought of these garments belonging to dead folk brought a little shudder to his spine, which was only right. This *was* Halloween, after all, and what was Halloween without a few chills?

After a few minutes of searching he found a long black coat with a collar he could turn up, which Wendell pronounced very vampiric. Well satisfied with his choice, he went back to the wall of faces, and his eyes almost immediately alighted upon a mask he hadn't previously seen, with the pallor and deep sockets of a soul just risen from the tomb. He took it down and put it on. It fitted perfectly.

"What do I look like?" Harvey asked, turning to face Wendell, who had found an executioner's mask which fitted him just as well.

"Ugly as sin."

"Good."

There was a flickering family of pumpkin heads lined up on the porch when they stepped outside, and the misty air smelled of wood smoke.

"Where do we go trick-or-treating?" Harvey wanted to know. "Out in the street?"

"No," said Wendell, "it's not Halloween out in the real world, remember? We're going to go around to the back of the House."

"That's not very far," Harvey remarked, disappointed.

"It is at this time of night," Wendell said creepily. "This House is full of surprises. You'll see."

Harvey looked up at the House through the tiny eyeholes of his mask. It loomed as large as a thunderhead, its weathervane sharp enough to stab the stars.

"Come on," said Wendell, "we've got a long trip ahead."

A long trip? Harvey thought; how could it be a long trip from the front of the House to the back? But once again Wendell was right: The House *was* full of surprises. The trip—which would have been a two-minute walk in the bright afternoon—soon became a trek that had Harvey wishing he'd brought a flashlight and a map. The leaves rustled underfoot as though snakes were swarming through them; the trees that had shaded them by day now looked frightful in their nakedness, gaunt and hungry.

"Why am I doing this?" he asked himself as he followed Wendell through the darkness. "I'm cold, and I'm uncomfortable." (He might have added *frightened* to the list, but he left that thought unsaid.)

As he was about to suggest they turn back, Wendell pointed up and hissed: "Look!"

Harvey looked. Directly overhead, a form was moving silently against the sky, as if it had just launched itself from the eaves of the House. The moon had slunk away behind the roof, and shed no light upon this night-flyer, so Harvey could only guess at its shape from the stars it blotted out as it sailed. Its wings were wide, but ragged—too ragged to bear it up, he thought. Instead it seemed to claw at the darkness as it went, as though it were crawling on the very air itself.

A glimpse was all Harvey had. Then it was gone.

"What *was* that?" he whispered.

He got no answer. In the moments he'd taken staring up at the sky, Wendell had disappeared.

"Wendell?" Harvey whispered. "Where are you?"

There was still no reply. Just the slithering in the leaves, and the moan of hungry branches.

"I know what you're doing," Harvey said, louder this time. "And you won't scare me that easy. Hear me?"

This time there *was* a reply of sorts. Not words, but a creaking sound from somewhere in the trees.

He's climbing up into the tree house, Harvey thought, and determined to catch Wendell and scare him back, he followed the sound.

Despite the nakedness of the branches, their mesh kept all but a glimmer of starlight from falling on the groves. He slipped his mask down around his neck so as to see a little better, but even then he was nearly blind, and had to listen out for the sound of Wendell's ascent to guide him. He could still hear the creaks plainly enough, and stumbled in their direction, his arms outstretched to grasp the ladder when he reached it.

Now the sound was so loud he was certain he must be standing beneath the tree. He looked up, hoping to catch a glimpse of the trickster, but as he did so something brushed his face. He snatched at it, but it was gone, at least for the moment. Then it came again, brushing his brow from the other side. He snatched at it a second time, then, as it touched him again, caught hold of it.

"Got you!" he cried.

His yell of triumph was followed by a rush of air, and the sound of something crashing to the ground at his side. He jumped, but refused to let go of whatever he was holding.

"Wendell?" he called.

By way of a reply a flame flared in the darkness behind him, and a firework erupted into a shower of green sparks, its light making a gangrenous cavern of the grove.

By its flickering light he saw what he held, and seeing, let out a panicked yammering that had the crows rising from their roosts overhead.

It was not a ladder he'd heard creaking, it was a rope. No, not even a rope: a *noose.* And in his hand, the leg of the man hanging from the noose. He let go of it and stumbled backward, barely suppressing a second shout as his eyes rose to meet the dead man's stare. To judge by his expression, he had died horribly. His tongue lolled from his foamy lips, his veins were so swollen with blood his head looked like a pumpkin.

Either that, or it *was* a pumpkin.

A fresh fountain of sparks now burst from the firework, and Harvey saw the truth of the matter. The limb he'd held was a stuffed trouser leg; the body a coat spilling bundles of

clothes; that head a mask on a pumpkin, with cream for spittle and eggs for eyes.

"Wendell!" he yelled, turning his back on this scene of execution.

Wendell was standing on the far side of the firework, his ear-to-ear grin lit by its spitting sparks. He looked like a little demon, fresh from the inferno. At his side was the ladder that had come crashing down to get the drama underway.

"I warned ya!" Wendell said, holding up his mask. "I said I was going to be a hangman tonight!"

"I'll get you back for this!" Harvey said, his heart still beating too fast for him to see the funny side of this. "I swear . . . I'll get you back!"

"You can try!" Wendell crowed. The firework was beginning to fizzle out; the shadows around them beginning to deepen again. "Had enough of Halloween for tonight?" he asked.

Harvey didn't much like admitting defeat, but he nodded grimly, swearing to himself that when he finally got his revenge, it would be choice.

"Smile," Wendell said, as the fountain of sparks dwindled. "We're in the Holiday House."

The light had almost gone, and even though Harvey was still enraged at Wendell (and at himself, for being such a sucker), he couldn't let it die away without making peace.

"All right," he said, allowing himself a tiny smile. "There'll be other nights."

"Always," said Wendell. The reply pleased him. "That's what this place is," he said, as the light went out. "It's the House of Always."

VII

A Present from the Past

THERE WAS A THANKSGIVING FEAST AWAITING THEM when they got back into the House.

"You look as though you've been in the wars," Mrs. Griffin remarked when she set eyes on Harvey. "Has Wendell been up to his tricks?"

Harvey admitted that he'd fallen for all of them, but there was one that impressed him in particular.

"What was that?" said Wendell with a smug grin. "The falling ladder? That *was* a clever little touch, wasn't it?"

"No, not the ladder," said Harvey.

"What then?"

"The thing in the sky."

"Oh that . . ."

"What was it? A kite?"

"That wasn't my doing," Wendell replied.

"What was it then?"

"I don't know," Wendell said, his smile disappearing. "Better not to ask, eh?"

"But I want to know," Harvey insisted, turning to Mrs. Griffin. "It had wings, and I think it flew off the roof."

"Then it was a bat," Mrs. Griffin said.

"No, this was a hundred times bigger than a bat." He spread his arms. "Great, dark wings."

Mrs. Griffin frowned as Harvey spoke. "You imagined it," she said.

"I did not," Harvey protested.

"Why don't you just sit down and eat?" Mrs. Griffin replied. "If it wasn't a bat then it wasn't anything at all."

"But Wendell saw it too. Didn't you Wendell?"

He looked around at the other boy, who was digging into a steaming plate of turkey and cranberry sauce.

"Who cares?" Wendell said, chewing as he spoke.

"Just tell her you saw it."

Wendell shrugged. "Maybe I did, maybe I didn't. It's Halloween night. There's supposed to be bogeymen out there."

"But not *real* ones," said Harvey. "A trick's one thing. But if that beast was *real* . . ."

As he spoke he realized he was breaking the rule he'd made on the porch: Whether the winged creature was real or not didn't matter. This was a place of illusions. Wouldn't he be happier here if he just stopped questioning what was real and what wasn't?

"Sit down and eat," Mrs. Griffin said again.

Harvey shook his head. His appetite had disappeared. He was angry, though he wasn't quite sure at whom. Maybe at Wendell, for his shrugs; or at Mrs. Griffin, for not believing him; or at himself, for being afraid of illusions. Maybe all three.

"I'm going up to my room to change," he said, and left the kitchen.

HE DISCOVERED LULU ON THE LANDING, STARING OUT the window. Wind gusted against the glass, reminding Harvey of Rictus's first visit. It wasn't rain the gusts were bringing, however, it was powdery snow.

"It'll be Christmas soon," she said.

"Will it?"

"There'll be presents for everyone. There always are. You should wish for something."

"Is that what you're doing?"

She shook her head. "No," she said. "I've been here so long I've got everything I ever wanted. Would you like to see?"

Harvey said yes, and she led him up the stairs to her room, which was immense, and filled with her treasures.

She obviously had a passion for boxes. Tiny, jeweled boxes; large, carved boxes. A box for her collection of glass balls; a box that played tinkling music; a box into which half a hundred smaller boxes fitted.

She also had several families of dolls, who sat in blank-faced rows around the walls. But more impressive by far was the house from which the dolls had been exiled. It stood in the middle of the room, five feet high from step to chimney top, every detail of brick, slate and sill perfect.

"This is where I keep my friends," Lulu said, and opened the front door.

Two bright green lizards came out to greet her, scurrying up her arms onto her shoulders.

"The rest are inside," she said. "Take a look."

Harvey peered through the windows, and found that every perfect room in the house was occupied. There were lizards lounging on the beds, lizards snoozing in the baths, lizards swinging from the chandeliers. He laughed out loud at their antics.

"Aren't they fun?" Lulu said.

"Great!" he replied.

"You can come up and play with them any time you want."

"Thanks."

"They're really very friendly. They only bite when they're hungry. Here—"

She plucked one off her shoulder and dropped it into Harvey's hands. It promptly ran up and perched on his head, much to Lulu's amusement.

They enjoyed the company of both the lizards and each other for a long while, until Harvey caught a glimpse of his reflection in one of the windows, and remembered what a sight he was.

"I'd better go and wash," he told Lulu. "I'll see you later."

She smiled at him. "I like you, Harvey Swick," she said.

Her honesty made *him* honest. "I like you too," he told her. Then, his expression darkening, he said: "I wouldn't want anything to happen to you."

She looked puzzled.

"I saw you at the lake," he said.

"Did you?" she replied. "I don't remember."

"Well anyway, it's deep. You should be careful. You could slip and fall in."

"I'll be careful," she said as he opened the door. "Oh, and Harvey—?"

"Yes?"

"Don't forget to wish for something."

WHAT SHALL I ASK FOR? HE WONDERED AS HE WASHED the dirt off his face. Something impossible maybe, to see just how much magic the House possessed. A white tiger, perhaps. A full-sized zeppelin? A ticket to the moon?

The answer came from the depths of his memory. He'd wish for a present he'd been given (and lost) a long time ago; a present that his father had made for him, which Mr. Hood, however much he might want to please his new guest, would never be able to duplicate.

"The ark," he murmured.

With his face washed, and the scratches he'd got from the thorns in the thicket worn like war wounds, he headed back downstairs, to find that once again the House had performed an extraordinary transformation. A Christmas tree—so tall that the star at its summit pricked the ceiling—stood in the hallway, the colors of its twinkling lights seeping into every room. There was a smell of chocolate in the air, and the sound of carols being sung. In the living room, Mrs. Griffin was sitting beside a roaring fire, with Stew-Cat purring on her lap.

"Wendell's gone outside," she told Harvey. "There's a scarf and gloves for you by the front door."

Harvey went out onto the porch. The wind was icy, but it was already clearing the snow clouds, leaving the stars to shine down on a perfect white carpet.

Not quite perfect. A trail of tracks led down from the House to the spot where Wendell was building a snowman.

"Coming out?" he hollered to Harvey, his voice as clear as the bells that were ringing through the crisp air.

Harvey shook his head. He was so tired even the snow looked comfortable.

"Maybe tomorrow," he said. "It'll be back tomorrow, won't it?"

"Of course," Wendell yelled. "And the night after, and the night after . . ."

Harvey went back inside to look at the Christmas tree. Its branches were hung with strings of popcorn and cranberries, with colored lights and baubles and soldiers in gleaming silver uniforms.

"There's something under there for you," Mrs. Griffin said, standing at the living room door. "I hope it's what you want, sweet."

Harvey knelt down and pulled a parcel with his name on it out from under the tree. His pulse quickened before he even opened it, because he knew from its shape, and from the way it rattled, that his wish had been answered. He pulled at the string, remembering as he did so how much littler his hands had been the first time he'd held this gift. The paper tore and fell away, and there, shiny and new, was a painted wooden ark.

It was a perfect copy of the one his father had made. The same yellow hull, the same orange prow, the same wheel-house with holes in its red roof for the giraffes to put their heads through. The same lead animals, all in pairs, snug in the hold or peering through the portholes: two dogs, two elephants, two camels, two doves; all these and a dozen more. And finally, the same little Noah with his square white beard, and his fat wife, complete with apron.

"How did he know?" Harvey murmured.

He hadn't intended the question to be heard, much less answered, but Mrs. Griffin said:

"Mr. Hood knows every dream in your head."

"But this is perfect," Harvey said in amazement. "Look, my dad ran out of blue paint when he was finishing the elephants, so one of them has blue eyes and the other one has green eyes. It's the same. It's exactly the same."

"Does it please you then?" Mrs. Griffin asked.

Harvey said it did, but that wasn't entirely the truth. It was eerie to have the ark back in his hands when he knew the real one had been lost; as though time had been turned on its heels, and he was a little kid again.

He heard Wendell stamping the snow off his feet at the front door, and was suddenly embarrassed to have such a childish present in his hands. He gathered it up in its wrapping and hurried away upstairs, intending to head back down for some supper.

But his bed looked too welcoming to be refused, and his stomach quite full enough for one night, so instead he closed the curtains on the gusty night and laid his head down on his pillow.

The Christmas bells were still ringing in some distant steeple, and their repetition lulled him into sleep. He dreamed that he was standing on the steps of his house, looking through the open door into its warm heart. Then the wind caught hold of him, turning him from the threshold, and carrying him away into a dreamless sleep.

VIII

Hungry Waters

THAT FIRST DAY IN THE HOLIDAY HOUSE, WITH ALL ITS seasons and its spectacles, set the pattern for the many that were to follow.

When Harvey woke the following morning, the sun was once again pouring through a crack in the curtains, but this time it lay in a warm pool on the pillow beside him. He sat up with a shout and a smile, and either one or the other (and sometimes both) remained on his lips for the rest of the day.

There was plenty to do. Work on the tree house in the spring morning, followed by food, and the laying of plans for the afternoon. Games and lazy hours in the heat of summer—sometimes with Wendell, sometimes with Lulu—then adventures by the light of a harvest moon. And finally, when the winter wind had blown out the flames in the pumpkin heads, and carpeted the grounds with snow, chilly fun for them all out in the frosty air, and a warm Christmas welcome when they were done.

It was a day of holidays, the third as fine as the second, and the fourth as fine as the third, and very soon Harvey began to forget that there was a dull world out beyond the wall, where the great beast February was still sleeping its tedious sleep.

His only real reminder of the life he'd left—besides a second telephone call he'd made to his mom and dad just to tell them all was well—was the present he'd wished for, and received, that first Christmas: his ark. He'd thought several times of trying it out on the lake, to see if it would float, but it wasn't until the afternoon of the seventh day that he got around to doing so.

Wendell had made a real glutton of himself at lunch, and had declared that it was far too hot to play, so Harvey wandered down to the lake on his own, with the ark tucked under his arm. He half expected—hoped, in fact—to find Lulu down there to keep him company, but the banks of the lake were empty.

Once he laid eyes on the gloomy waters he almost gave up on the idea of a launching, but that meant admitting something to himself that he didn't wish to admit, so he headed on down to the shore, found a rock to perch on that looked less precarious than the others, and set his ark on the water.

It floated well, he was pleased to see. He pushed it to and fro for a little while, then lifted it out and peered inside to see if it was leaking. It was quite watertight, however, so he set it back on the lake and pushed it out again.

As he did so, he caught sight of a fish rising from the bottom of the lake, its mouth wide open, as if it intended to swallow his little vessel whole. He reached out to snatch the ark from the water before it was either sunk or devoured, but in his haste he lost his footing on the slime-slickened rock, and with a cry he fell into the lake.

The water was icy cold, and eager. It quickly closed over his head. He flailed wildly, trying not to imagine the dark depths beneath him, or the vast maw of the fish that had been rising from those depths. Turning his face up toward the surface, he started to swim.

He could see his ark floating above him, capsized by his fall. Its lead passengers were already sinking. He didn't try and save them, but surfaced—gasping for breath—and paddled toward the shore. It wasn't much of a distance. In less than a minute he was hauling himself up onto the rocks and scrambling away from the bank, water pouring from his sleeves and trousers and shoes. Only when his feet were clear of the lake, and no hungry fish could snap at his toes, did he drop down onto the ground.

Though it was midsummer, and the sun was blazing somewhere overhead, the air around the lake was cold, and he soon began to shiver. Before he made his way out into the sun, however, he looked for some sign of his ark. The spot where it had sunk was marked by a forlorn flotilla of wreckage, all of which would soon join the rest of the ark at the bottom.

Of the fish that had seemed so eager to devour him there was no sign. Perhaps it had swum down into the depths to chew on the drowned menagerie. If so, Harvey hoped it choked on its dinner.

He'd lost plenty of toys before. He'd had a brand new bicycle—his prize possession!—stolen from the step of his house two birthdays ago. But this loss upset him as much; more, in fact. The idea that the lake now had something that he'd owned was somehow worse than a thief running off with his bike. A thief was warm flesh and blood; the lake was not. His possessions had gone into a nightmare place, full of monstrous things, and he felt as though a little part of himself had gone with it, down into the dark.

He walked away from the lake without looking back, but the breeze that came to warm his face when he broke through the thicket, and the sound of birds that pleased his ear, could not keep from his mind the thought he'd tried to ignore when he'd gone down to the water. Despite all entertainments that the Holiday House supplied so eagerly, it was a haunted place, and however hard he had tried to ignore his doubts and suppress his questions, they could be ignored and suppressed no longer. Whoever, or *whatever,* that haunter was, Harvey could not be content now until he'd seen its face and knew its nature.

IX

What Do You Dream?

Harvey didn't mention what had happened at the lake to anyone—not even Lulu—in part because he felt stupid for falling in and in part because the House tried so hard to please him in the days that followed that he almost forgot about the accident entirely. That very night, in fact, he found a piece of colored string with his name tag on it at the base of the Christmas tree, and followed it through the House to find a new bike—even more splendid than the one he'd lost two years before—waiting for him.

But that was just the first of many fine surprises the Holiday House sprang in quick succession. One morning, for instance, Wendell and Harvey climbed up into the tree house to discover that the branches around it were swarming with parrots and monkeys. Another day, in the middle of Thanksgiving dinner, Mrs. Griffin called them through into the living room, where the flames of the fire had taken on the shapes of dragons and heroes, and were doing fiery battle in the grate. And in the heat of one lazy afternoon, Harvey was wakened from a doze by a chorus of shouts and found a troupe of mechanical acrobats performing clockwork-defying feats on the lawn.

The greatest surprise, however, began with the appearance of one of Rictus's siblings.

"My name is Jive," he said, stepping out of the early evening murk at the top of the stairs. Every muscle in his body seemed to be in motion: tics, jigs and jitterings that had wasted him away until he barely cast a shadow. Even his hair, which was a mass of oiled curls, seemed to hear some crazed rhythm. It writhed on his scalp in a knotted frenzy.

"Brother Rictus sent me along to see how you're doin'," he said, his tones succulent.

"I'm doing fine," Harvey replied. "Did you say *Brother Rictus*?"

"We're from the same brood, loosely speaking," Jive said. "I hope you call your folks now and then."

"Yep," said Harvey. "I called them yesterday."

"Are they missin' you?"

"Didn't sound like it."

"Are *you* missin' *them*?"

Harvey shrugged. "Not really," he said.

(This wasn't strictly true—he had his homesick days—but he knew if he went back home he'd be in school the day after, and wishing he'd stayed in the Holiday House a while longer.)

"You're going to make the most of bein' here then?" said Jive, practicing a weird little dance step up and down the stairs.

"Yeah," said Harvey. "I just want to have fun."

"Who doesn't?" Jive grinned, "who doesn't?" He sidled up to Harvey, and whispered: "Speakin' of fun . . ."

"What?" said Harvey.

"You never *did* get Wendell back for that trick of his."

"No, I didn't," said Harvey.

"Why the heck not?"

"I could never think of a way."

"Oh I'm sure we could cook something up between the two of us," Jive replied mischievously.

"It has to be something he'll never think of," Harvey said.

"That shouldn't be difficult," said Jive. "Tell me, what's your favorite monster?"

Harvey didn't have to think hard about that. "A vampire," he said with a grin. "I found this great mask—"

"Masks are a good beginning," Jive said, "but vampires need to swoop out of the mist—" he spread his arms, curling his long fingers like the claws of some eye-gouging beast

"—swoop down, snatch up their prey, then rise up again, up against the moon. I can see it now."

"So can I," said Harvey. "But I'm not a bat."

"So?"

"So how do I swoop?"

"Ah," said Jive. "We'll have Marr work on that for us. After all, what's a Halloween without a transformation or two?" He consulted the grandfather clock on the landing. "We've still got time to do it tonight. You go down and tell Wendell you'll meet him outside. I'll go up onto the roof and find Marr. You meet us up there."

"I've never been up on the roof."

"There's a door on the top landing. I'll see you up there in a few minutes."

"I'll have to get my mask an' coat an' stuff."

"You won't need a mask tonight," Jive said, "trust me. Now you hurry up. Time's a-wastin'."

It took Harvey only a minute or two to tell Wendell to go on ahead. He was sure Wendell suspected something, and was probably preparing some counterattack, but Harvey knew he and Jive had something up their sleeves even Wendell—expert on shock tactics though he was—couldn't anticipate. With the first part of the plan laid he hurried upstairs again, found the door Jive had mentioned, and climbed up onto the roof.

Heights had never bothered him; he liked to be up above the world looking down on it.

"Over here!" Jive called to him, and Harvey took off along the narrow walkways and up the steep roofs to where his fellow conspirator stood.

"Sure-footed!" Jive observed.

"No problem."

"How 'bout flyin'?" said a third voice, as its owner stepped from the shadows of a chimney.

"This is Marr," Jive said. "Another of our little family."

Unlike Jive, who looked nimble enough to walk on the eaves if the whim took him, Marr seemed to have slug blood in her somewhere. Harvey almost expected to see her fingers leave silver trails on the brick she touched, or see soft horns appear from her balding head. She was grossly fat, her flesh barely clinging to her bones. Wherever it could—around her mouth and eyes, at her neck and wrists—it collapsed in clammy folds. She reached out and poked Harvey.

"I said: What 'bout flyin'?"

"What about it?" Harvey said, pushing her hand away.

"Done much?"

"I flew to Florida once."

"She doesn't mean in a plane," Jive told him.

"Oh . . ."

"In dreams maybe?" said Marr.

"Oh yeah, I dream about flying."

"That's good," Marr replied, grinning with satisfaction. She had not a single tooth in her mouth.

Harvey stared at the empty maw in disgust.

"You're wondering where they've gone, aren't you?" she said to Harvey. "Go on. Admit it."

Harvey shrugged. "Well yes. I am."

"Carna took them, the thieving brute. I had fine teeth. Beautiful teeth."

"Who's Carna?" Harvey wanted to know.

"Never mind," Jive said, hushing Marr before she could reply. "Get to it or he'll miss the moment."

Marr muttered something beneath her breath, then said: "Come to me, boy," extending her arms in Harvey's direction. Her touch was icy.

"Feels weird, huh?" said Jive, as Marr's fingers floated over his face, brushing it here and there. "Don't worry. She knows what she's doin'."

"And what's that?"

"Changin' you."

"Into what?"

"You tell her," Jive said. "It won't last long, so enjoy it. Go on, tell her about being a vampire."

"That's what I want Wendell to see," Harvey said.

"A vampire . . ." Marr said softly, her fingers pressing harder against his skin.

"Yeah, I want to have fangs, like a wolf, and a red throat, and white skin, like I've been dead for a thousand years."

"Two thousand!" said Jive.

"Ten thousand!" said Harvey, beginning to enjoy the game. "And crazy eyes, that can see in the dark, and pointy ears, like a bat's ears—"

"Wait up!" Marr said. "I've got to get all this right."

Her fingers were working hard upon him now, as though his flesh was clay, and she was molding it. His face was tingling, and he wanted to reach up and touch it, but he was afraid of spoiling her handiwork.

"And there's got to be fur," Jive observed. "Sleek, black fur on his neck—"

Marr's hands dabbled at his throat, and he felt fur sprouting where she'd touched him.

"—and the wings!" Harvey said. "Don't forget the wings!"

"Never!" said Jive.

"Spread your arms, boy," Marr told him.

He did so, and she ran her hands along them, smiling now.

"It's good," she said. "It's good."

He looked down at himself. To his astonishment he found his fingers were gnarled and sharp, and leathery flaps were hanging from his arms. The wind gusted against them, threatening to carry him off the roof then and there.

"You know you're playin' a dangerous game, don't you?" Marr said as she stood back to admire her handiwork. "You'll either break your head or scare the life out of your friend Wendell. Or both."

"He won't fall, woman!" Jive said. "He's got the knack of this. I can tell just by looking at him." He peered at Harvey with his squinty eyes. "Wouldn't be surprised if you weren't a vampire in another life, boy," he said.

"Vampires don't *have* other lives," Harvey said, the words more difficult to say with a mouthful of fangs. "They live forever."

"That's right," said Jive, snapping his fingers. "So they do! So they do!"

"Well, I'm finished," said Marr. "You can get goin', boy."

The wind came gusting again, and if Jive hadn't been holding on to him as they walked the edge of the roof, Harvey would surely have been carried away.

"There's your friend," Jive whispered, pointing down into the shadows.

Much to his amazement Harvey found that he could see Wendell quite clearly, even though it was pitch dark in the thicket. He could hear him too: every little breath, every beat of his heart.

"This is it," Jive hissed, putting his hand on Harvey's back.

"What do I do?" Harvey said. "Do I flap or what?"

"Jump!" Jive said. "The wind'll take care of the rest. Either the wind or gravity."

And with that, he shoved Harvey off the edge of the roof and into the empty air.

X

Falling from Grace

THE WIND WASN'T THERE TO BEAR HIM UP. HE PLUM-meted like a slate tossed from the gables, a cry of sheer terror escaping his throat. He saw Wendell turn; saw a look of mortal fear come onto his face; then the wind came out of nowhere, cold and strong, and just as his legs brushed the bushes he felt himself lifted up and up, toward the sky.

His cry became a whoop; his terror, joy. The moon was larger than he'd ever seen it, and its vast white face filled his sight, like the face of his mother, bending to kiss him good night.

Except that he needed no sleep tonight, no, nor a mother to wish him sweet dreams. This was better than any dream, flying with the wind in his wings, and the world shuddering below in fear of his shadow.

He looked for Wendell again, and saw him fleeing for the safety of the House.

No you don't, he thought, and turning his wings like leathery sails he swooped down on his prey. A bloodcurdling shriek filled his ears, and for a moment he thought it was the wind. Then he realized it was his own throat that was uttering this inhuman din, and the shriek became laughter; wild, luna-tic laughter.

"Don't ... please ... *don't!*" Wendell was sobbing as he ran. "Somebody help me! Somebody help me!"

Harvey knew he'd already had his revenge: Wendell was frightened out of his wits. But it was too much fun to stop now. He liked the feel of the wind beneath him, and the cold moon on his back. He liked the sharpness of his eyes, and the strength of his claws. But most of all he liked the fear he was causing; liked the look on Wendell's upturned face, and the sound of panic in his chest.

The wind was carrying him down into the thicket, and as he landed Wendell dropped to his knees, begging for mercy.

"Don't kill me! Please, *please,* I beg you—*don't kill me!*"

Harvey had seen and heard enough. He'd had his revenge. It was time to put an end to the game, before the fun soured.

He opened his mouth to announce himself, but Wendell— seeing the red throat and the wolfish fangs, and thinking this meant certain death—began a new round of supplications. This time, however, he wasn't simply begging.

"I'm too fat to eat," he said. "But there's another kid around here somewhere—"

Harvey growled at this.

"There is!" Wendell said. "I swear. And there's more meat on him than on me!"

"Listen to the child," said a voice in the bushes at Harvey's side. He glanced around. There was Jive, his wiry form barely visible among the barbs. "He'd see you dead, young Harvey."

Wendell heard none of this. He was still advertising the edibility of his friend, hoisting up his shirt and shaking his blubbery belly to prove how unpalatable he was.

"You don't want me . . ." he sobbed. "Take Harvey! Take Harvey!"

"*Bite him,*" said Jive. "Go on. Drink a little of his blood. Why not? The fat's no good, but the blood's hot, the blood's tasty." He was doing a little dance as he spoke, stamping his feet to the rhythm of his chant. "Don't waste the taste! Go eat the meat!"

And still Wendell whined, all snot and tears. "You don't want me. Find Harvey! Find Harvey!"

And the more he sobbed, the more Jive's chant made sense

to Harvey. Who was this ridiculous boy Wendell anyway? He was too eager to serve Harvey up as dinner to be called a friend. He was just a tasty morsel. Any vampire worth his wings would chew off his head as soon as look at him. And yet . . .

"What are you waiting for?" Jive wanted to know. "We've gone to all this trouble to make a monster of you—"

"Yes, but it's a game," Harvey said.

"A game?" said Jive. "No, no, boy. It's more than that. It's an *education*."

Harvey didn't know what he meant by this, and he wasn't altogether certain he *wanted* to know.

"If you don't pounce soon," Jive hissed, "you're going to lose him."

It was true. Wendell's tears were clearing, and he was staring at his attacker with a puzzled look.

"Are you . . . going to let me . . . go?" he murmured.

Harvey felt Jive's hand on his back.

"Do it!" Jive said.

Harvey looked at Wendell's tear-stained face and trembling hands. If the situation had been reversed, he thought to himself, would I have been much braver? The answer, he knew, was no.

"It's now or never," said Jive.

"Then it's never," Harvey said. *"Never!"*

The word came out as a guttural roar, and Wendell fled before it, yelling at the top of his voice. Harvey didn't give chase.

"You disappoint me, boy," Jive said. "I thought you had the killer instinct."

"Well, I don't," said Harvey, a little ashamed of himself. He felt like a coward, even though he knew he'd done the right thing.

"That was a waste of magic," said another voice, and Marr appeared from out of the bushes, her arms filled with enormous fungi.

"Where'd you find those?" Jive said.

"Usual place," Marr replied. She gave Harvey a contemptuous look. "I suppose you want your old body back," she said.

"Yes, please."

"We should leave him like this," said Jive. "He'd get around to sucking blood sooner or later."

"Nah," said Marr. "There's only so much magic to go around, you know that. Why waste it on a miserable little punk like this?"

She waved her hand casually in Harvey's direction, and he felt the power that had filled his limbs and transformed his face drain out of him. It was a relief, of course, to feel the magic unmade, but a little part of him mourned the loss. In a matter of moments he was once again an earthbound boy, wingless and weak.

With the spell removed, Marr turned her back on him and waddled off into the darkness. Jive, however, lingered long enough to have one last dig at Harvey.

"You missed your chance there, kiddo," he said. "You could have been one of the greats."

"It was a trick, that's all," Harvey said, concealing the strange unhappiness he felt. "A Halloween trick. It meant nothing."

"There are those who'd disagree," Jive said darkly. "Those who'd say that all the great powers in the world are *bloodsuckers* and *soul-stealers* at heart. And we must serve them. All of us. Serve them to our dying day."

He stared hard at Harvey all the way through this peculiar little speech, and then, with a nimble step, retreated into the shadows and was gone.

Harvey found Wendell in the kitchen, a hot dog in one

hand and a cookie in the other, telling Mrs. Griffin about what he'd seen. He dropped his food when Harvey came in, and yelped with relief: "You're alive! You're alive!"

"Of *course* I'm alive," said Harvey. "wWhy shouldn't I be?"

"There was something *out* there. A terrible beast. It almost ate me. I thought maybe it had eaten you."

Harvey looked down at his hands and legs.

"Nope," he said. "Not a nibble."

"I'm glad!" Wendell said. "I'm so, so glad. You're my best friend, for always."

I was vampire food five minutes ago, Harvey thought, but he said nothing. Maybe there'd come a time when he could tell Wendell about his transformation and temptation, but this wasn't it. He simply said:

"I'm hungry," and sat down at the table beside his fair-weather friend, to put something sweeter than blood in his belly.

XI

Turnabout

NEITHER WENDELL NOR LULU WAS AROUND THE FOL-
lowing day—Mrs. Griffin said she'd seen them both before
breakfast, and then they'd disappeared—so Harvey was left to
his own devices. He tried not to think about what had happened the night before, but he couldn't help himself.

Snatches of conversation kept coming back, and he puzzled over them all day long. What had Jive meant, for instance,
when he'd told Harvey that turning him into a vampire was
not so much a *game* as an *education?* What kind of lesson had
he learned by jumping off a roof and scaring Wendell?

And all that stuff about soul-stealers and how they had
to be *served;* what had that meant? Was it Mr. Hood that Jive
had been speaking of; that *great power* they all had to serve?
If Hood was somewhere in the House, why hadn't anyone—
Lulu, Wendell or himself—encountered him? Harvey had
quizzed his friends about Hood, and had the same story from
them both: They'd heard no footfalls, no whispers, no laughter.
If Mr. Hood was indeed here, *where* was he hiding, and *why?*

So many questions; so few answers.

And then, as if these mysteries weren't enough, another
came along to vex him. In the late afternoon, lounging in the
shade of the tree house, he heard a yell of frustration, and peered
through the leaves to see Wendell racing across the lawn. He was
dressed in a windbreaker and boots, even though it was swelter-
ingly hot, and he was stamping around like a madman.

Harvey shouted to him, but his call went either unheard
or ignored, so he climbed down and pursued Wendell around

the side of the House. He found him in the orchard, red-faced and sweaty.

"What's going on?" he said.

"I can't get out!" Wendell said, grinding a half-rotted apple underfoot. "I want to leave, Harvey, but there's no way out!"

"Of course there is!"

"I've been trying for hours and hours and I tell you the mist keeps sending me back the way I came."

"Hey, calm down!"

"I want to go home, Harvey," Wendell said, close to tears now. "Last night was too much for me. That thing came after my blood. I know you don't believe me—"

"I do," said Harvey, "honest I do."

"You do?"

"For sure."

"Well, then maybe you should leave too, 'cause if *I* go it'll come after *you*."

"I don't think so," said Harvey.

"I've been kiddin' myself about this place," Wendell said. "It's *dangerous*. Oh, yeah, I know it seems like everything's perfect, but—"

Harvey interrupted him. "Maybe you should keep your voice down," he said. "We should talk about this *quietly*. In private."

"Like where?" said Wendell, wild-eyed. "The whole place is watching us and listening to us. Don't you feel it?"

"Why would it do that?"

"I don't know!" Wendell snapped. "But last night I thought, if I don't leave I'm going to die here. I'll just disappear one night; or go crazy like Lulu." He dropped his voice to a whisper. "We're not the first, you know. What about all the clothes upstairs? All the coats and shoes and hats. They belonged to kids like us."

Harvey shuddered. Had he played trick-or-treat in a murdered boy's shoes?

"I want to get out of here," Wendell said, tears running down his face. "But there's no way out."

"If there's a way *in* there must be a way *out*," Harvey reasoned. "We'll go to the wall."

With that he marched off, Wendell in tow, around to the front of the House and down the gentle slope of the lawn. The mist-wall looked perfectly harmless as they approached it.

"Be careful—" Wendell warned. "It's got some tricks up its sleeve."

Harvey slowed his step, expecting the wall to twitch, or even reach for him. But it did nothing. Bolder now, he strode into the mist, fully expecting to emerge on the other side. But by some trick or other he was turned around without even being aware of it, and delivered out of the wall with the House in front of him.

"What happened?" he said to himself. Puzzled, he stepped back into the mist.

The same thing occurred. In he went, and out he came again, facing the opposite direction. He tried again, and again, and again, but the same trick was worked upon him every time, until Harvey was as frustrated as Wendell had been a half hour before.

"*Now* do you believe me?" Wendell said.

"Yep."

"So what do we do?"

"Well, we don't yell about it," Harvey whispered. "We just get on with the day. Pretend we've given up leaving. I'm going to do a little looking around."

HE BEGAN HIS INVESTIGATIONS AS SOON AS THEY GOT back into the House, by going in search of Lulu. Her bedroom door was closed. He knocked, then called her. There was no reply, so he tried the handle. The door was unlocked.

"Lulu?" he called. "It's Harvey."

She wasn't there, but he was relieved to see that her bed had been slept in, and that she'd apparently been playing with her pets recently. The doors to the doll's house were open, and the lizards were everywhere underfoot.

There was one strangeness, however. The sound of running water led him through to the bathroom, where he found the bath full almost to brimming, and Lulu's clothes scattered in the puddles on the tile.

"Have you seen Lulu?" he asked Mrs. Griffin when he got downstairs.

"Not in the last few hours," she replied. "But she's been keeping to herself." Mrs. Griffin looked hard at Harvey. "I wouldn't pay too much mind if I were you, child," she said. "Mr. Hood doesn't like inquisitive guests."

"I was only wondering where she'd got to," Harvey said.

Mrs. Griffin frowned, her tongue working against her pale cheek as though it wanted to speak, but didn't dare.

"Anyway," Harvey went on, deliberately goading Mrs. Griffin, "I don't believe Mr. Hood *exists*."

"Now you be careful," she said, her voice and frown deepening. "You don't want to talk about Mr. Hood that way."

"I've been here . . . days and days," Harvey said, realizing as he spoke that he'd lost count of his time in the House. "And I haven't seen him once. *Where is he?*"

Now Mrs. Griffin came at Harvey with her hands raised, and for a moment he thought she was going to strike him. But instead she took hold of his shoulders and shook him.

"*Please,* child!" she said. "Be content with what you know. You're here to enjoy yourself for a little time. And child, it's *such* a little time. It flies by. Oh Lord, how it flies!"

"It's just a few weeks," Harvey said. "I'm not going to stay here forever." Now it was *he* who stared at *her*. "Or am I?" he said.

"Stop," she told him.

"You think I *am* here forever, don't you?" he said, shaking off her grip. "What *is* this place, Mrs. Griffin? Is it some kind of prison?"

She shook her head.

"Don't tell me lies," he said. "It's stupid. We're locked up in here, aren't we?"

Now, though she was shaking with fear from head to foot, she dared to make a tiny nod of her head.

"All of us?" he asked. Again she nodded. "You too?"

"Yes," she whispered, "me too. And there's no way out. Believe me, if you try to escape again, Carna will come after you."

"Carna..." he said, remembering the name from the conversation between Jive and Marr.

"He's up there," Mrs. Griffin said. "On the roof. That's where the four of them live. Rictus, Marr, Carna—"

"—and Jive."

"You know."

"I've met them all but Carna."

"Pray you never do," said Mrs. Griffin. "Now listen to me, Harvey. I've seen many children come and go through this House—some of them foolish, some of them selfish, some sweet, some brave—but you, you are one of the brightest souls I have ever set eyes on. I want you to take what joy you can from being here. Use the hours well, because there'll be fewer than you think."

Harvey listened patiently to this. Then, when she'd finished, he said: "I still want to meet Mr. Hood."

"Mr. Hood is dead," Mrs. Griffin said, exasperated by his persistence.

"Dead? You swear?"

"I swear," she replied. "On the grave of my poor Clue-Cat, I swear: *Mr. Hood is dead.* So don't ask about him ever again."

This was the first time Mrs. Griffin had ever come close to giving Harvey an order, and though he wanted to press her further, he decided not to. Instead he said he was sorry for bringing up the subject, and wouldn't do it again, then left her to her secret sorrows.

XII

What the Flood Gave Up (and What It Took)

W ELL?" SAID WENDELL, WHEN HARVEY CAME TO HIS
room. "What's the story?"

Harvey shrugged. "Everything's fine," he said. "Why
don't we just enjoy ourselves while we can?"

"Enjoy ourselves?" Wendell said. "How can we enjoy ourselves when we're locked in?"

"It's better in here than it is out in the world," Harvey said.
Wendell looked at him in astonishment. "That's true isn't it?"

As he spoke he grabbed hold of Wendell's hand, and Wendell realized there was a ball of paper in Harvey's palm, which
he was trying to pass between the two of them.

"Maybe you should just find a quiet little corner and do
some reading," he said, glancing down at their hands as he
spoke.

Wendell got the idea. He claimed the balled-up note from
Harvey's hand and said: "Maybe I'll do that."

"Good," said Harvey. "I'm going to go out and enjoy the
sun while I can."

That was exactly what he did. He had a lot of planning to
do before midnight, which was when the note told Wendell
they should meet to make their escape. Surely even the forces
that guarded the House had to sleep sometime (the business of
keeping the seasons rolling around couldn't be easy) and of all
the hours to slip away, midnight seemed the most promising.

But he didn't suppose it would be easy. The House had
been a trap for decades (perhaps centuries: Who knew how old
its evil really was?) and even at midnight it would not be so
foolish as to leave the exit wide open. They would have to be

quick and clever, and not panic or lose their tempers once they were in the mist. The real world was out there somewhere. All they had to do was find it.

HE KNEW WHEN HE SAW WENDELL FOR HALLOWEEN that the note had been read and understood. There was a look in Wendell's eyes that said: I'm ready. I'm nervous, but I'm ready.

The rest of the evening passed for the two of them like the performance of a strange play, in which they were the actors, and the House (or whoever haunted it) was the audience. They went about enjoying themselves as though this was a night like any other, heading out to play trick-or-treat with a show of loud laughter (even though they were both shuddering in their borrowed shoes), then coming in to eat their supper and spend what they hoped would be their last Christmas in the House. They opened their presents (a mechanical dog for Wendell; a magician's kit for Harvey), said their good nights to Mrs. Griffin (good-*bye*, of course, not good *night*, but Harvey didn't dare let her know) and then went to bed.

The House grew quiet, and quieter still. The snow no longer sighed at the sill, nor the wind in the chimney. It was, Harvey thought, the deepest silence he'd ever heard; so deep that he could hear his heartbeat in his ears, and every rustle of his body against the sheets sounded like a roll of drums.

A little before midnight he got up and dressed, moving slowly and carefully, so as to make as little noise as possible. Then he headed out into the passageway, and—slipping like a thief from shadow to shadow—hurried down the stairs and out into the night.

He left not by the front door (it was heavy, and creaked loudly) but by the kitchen door, which brought him out at the side of the House. Though the wind had dropped, the air was still bitter and the surface of the snow had frozen. It crackled as he walked, however lightly he trod. But he was beginning to hope that the eyes and ears of the House were indeed closed at this hour (if not, why hadn't he been challenged?) and he might make it to the perimeter without attracting attention.

Just as he was about to turn the corner, however, that sweet hope was soured, as somebody in the murk behind him called his name. He froze in his tracks, hoping the darkness would conceal him, but the voice came again, and again called his name. It was not a voice he recognized. Not Wendell, certainly, nor Mrs. Griffin. Not Jive, not Rictus, not Marr. This was a frail voice; the voice of somebody who barely knew how to shape the syllables of his name.

"Harrr... vvvey..."

And then, all of a sudden, he knew the voice, and his heart—which had been working overtime since he'd slipped out of bed—grew so loud in his ears it almost drowned out the summons when it came again.

"Lulu?" he murmured.

"Yesss..." said the voice.

"Where are you?"

"Near..." she said.

He stared at the thicket, hoping for some glimpse of her, but all he could see was the starlight glittering on the frosted leaves.

"You're leaving..." she said, her words slurred.

"Yes," he whispered, "and you have to come with us."

He took a step toward her, and as he did so some of the glitter that he'd thought was frost retreated from him. What was she wearing, that shimmered this way?

"Don't be afraid," he said.

"I don't want you to look at me," she said.

"What's wrong?"

"Please..." she said, "just... keep your distance..."

She retreated even farther from him, and seemed to lose

her balance as she did so. She dropped to the ground, the thicket around her shaking. Harvey stepped forward to help her up, but she let out such a sob that he stopped in his tracks.

"I only want to help," he said.

"You can't help me," she replied, every word pained. "It's too late. You just have . . . to go . . . while you still can. I just . . . wanted to give you . . . something to remember me by."

He saw her move in the shadows, reaching out in his direction.

"Look away," she said.

He turned his head away from her.

"Now close your eyes. And promise you won't open them."

He dutifully closed his eyes. "I promise," he said.

And now he heard her moving toward him, her breath laborious.

"Open your hand," she said.

Her voice was near now. He knew if he opened his eyes he'd be face to face with her. But he had made a promise, and was determined to keep it. He put out his hand and felt first one, then two, then three heavy little objects, cold and wet, dropped into his cupped palm.

"This was all . . . I could find . . ." Lulu said, ". . . I'm sorry . . ."

"Can I look?" he asked.

"Not yet. Let me . . . leave . . . first . . ."

He closed his fingers around the gifts she'd given him, trying to make sense of them by touch. What were they? Pieces of frozen stone? No, they were carved. He could feel grooves on one; a head on another. And now, of course, he knew what he held: three survivors of his ark, dredged up from the depths of the lake.

The answer was no comfort to him; quite the reverse. He shuddered as he put the puzzle of Lulu's silvery gleam together with the knowledge of what he held. She had swum down to the bottom of the lake to recover these figures, a descent that was beyond the capacity of any land dweller.

No wonder she'd retreated into the shadows, ordering him not to look at her. She wasn't human any longer. She was becoming—or had already become—a sister to the strange fish that circled in these dark waters, cold-blooded and silver-skinned.

"Oh, Lulu . . ." he said, ". . . how did this happen?"

"Don't waste your time with me," she murmured, "just go while you've a chance."

"I want to help," he said.

"You can't . . ." came the reply, ". . . can't help me . . . I've been here too long. My life is over . . ."

"That's not true," Harvey said. "We're the same age."

"But I've been here so long I don't even remember . . ." Her voice trailed away.

"Don't remember *what?*"

"Maybe I just don't *want* to remember," she said. "It'll hurt too much . . ." She made a long, choked sigh. "You have to go . . ." she said in a whisper, ". . . go while you still can."

"I'm not afraid."

"Then you're *stupid,*" she said. "Because you should be."

He heard the thicket shake as she started to retreat from him.

"Wait," he said. She made no reply. *"Lulu!"*

The din of her departure grew louder. By the sound of it she was almost throwing herself out of his range. Breaking his promise, he opened his eyes, and caught a glimpse of her as she fled; a shadow in the shadows, no more. He started after her, not knowing what he would say or do when he caught up with her, but knowing he'd never forgive himself if he didn't somehow help.

Maybe if he persuaded her to go with him, out of the shadow of the House, its vicious magic would be undone. Or maybe he could find some doctor for her in the outside world who could cure her of this malformation. Anything rather than leaving her to return to the lake.

Its waters were in view now, gleaming darkly between the branches of the thicket. Lulu had reached the bank, and for a moment the meager starlight found her. All that Harvey had feared was true, and more. A fin grew from her bent and scaly back, and her legs had almost fused together. Her arms had become short and stubby, her fingers webbed.

But it was her face, glimpsed as she turned back to look at him, that was the greatest shock.

Her hair had fallen out, and her nose disappeared. Her mouth had lost its lips and her blue eyes turned to swivelling silver balls, lidless and lashless. And yet, despite their freak-ishness, there was human feeling in those eyes, and on that mouth: a terrible sadness that he knew would never leave his heart if he lived to be a thousand.

"You were my friend," she said as she teetered on the bank. "Thank you for that."

Then she tumbled into the water.

He went to the edge of the lake at a dash, but by the time he reached the place from which she'd dived the ripples were disappearing and the bubbles breaking. He watched the icy waters for a minute or more, hoping she would see him and surface, but she'd gone where he couldn't follow, and that, it seemed, was the end of it.

Clutching her gifts to him like talismans, he trudged away from the lake and down the lawn to keep his rendezvous with Wendell.

XIII

The Fourth Part of Darkness

WHAT HAPPENED TO YOU?" WENDELL WHISPERED when Harvey reached the bottom of the lawn. "I thought we were meeting at midnight."

"I got . . . waylaid," Harvey said.

He'd intended to tell Wendell what had just transpired, but his friend was obviously nervous enough without being told about Lulu's fate. Harvey slipped the three survivors of the ark into his pocket and resolved only to speak of the encounter when he and Wendell were safely away from this terrible place.

Just one thing stood between them and that ambition: the wall of mist. Now, as ever, it seemed innocent enough. But that was an illusion, of course, like so many things in Mr. Hood's kingdom.

"We have to be very organized about this," Harvey said to Wendell. "Once we're in the wall we lose our sense of direction. So we have to be sure we keep walking in a straight line, and not let the mist turn us around."

"How do we do that?" said Wendell.

"I think one of us should go in first, and the other one keep hold of his hand."

"Me," said Wendell, eagerly. "I want to be first."

"No problem. Then I'll keep my back to the House, and keep guiding you. Who knows, maybe the wall's so thin you'll just be able to pull me through."

"We can hope," Wendell said.

"Are you ready?" Harvey asked, extending his hand.

Wendell took it. "Whenever you are," he said.

"Then let's get out of here."

Wendell nodded, and stepped into the mist. Instantly, Harvey felt his grip tighten.

"Don't . . . let . . . go . . ." Wendell said, his voice already remote although he was just a pace away.

"Just keep walking," Harvey said, as they reached arm's length. "Any sign of—"

Before he could finish his question a noise from the House behind him sealed his lips. He glanced back. The front door was open, and a light was burning in the hall, throwing into silhouette the figure rushing down the porch steps. It was Mrs. Griffin.

The noise he'd heard was not from her lips, however. Nothing human could make such a din. He saw Mrs. Griffin glance up toward the roof as she hurried down the lawn, and following her gaze, saw the noise-maker rising against the stars.

He knew its name, even though he couldn't see its face. Hood had four servants, and he'd met only three: Rictus, Jive and Marr. Here was the fourth: Carna, the tooth-stealer; Carna, the devourer; Carna, the beast Mrs. Griffin had hoped Harvey would never meet.

"Back to the House, child!" Mrs. Griffin yelled as the din of vast wings filled the air. *"Quickly! Quickly!"*

Harvey pulled on Wendell's arm, yelling to him as he did so, but Wendell had a whiff of freedom in his nostrils and wasn't about to give it up.

"What are you waiting for?" Mrs. Griffin yelled. "Get away from there or it'll take off your head!"

Harvey glanced up at the swooping beast, and knew this was no lie. Carna's jaws were wide enough to snap him in half with a single bite. But he couldn't leave Wendell in the mist. They'd begun this adventure together, and that was how they would finish it, dead or alive. He had no choice but to step into the mist himself, and hope that Wendell had snatched a glimpse of the world outside, and could pull him through to the street.

As he took that step, he heard Mrs. Griffin say something about leading the way; then he was blinded by the chill of the mist, and the sound of her voice became a garbled whisper.

Carna's shrieks were not so hushed, however. They pierced the murk, skewering Harvey's thoughts the way its teeth would skewer his head if the beast caught up with him.

"Wendell?" Harvey yelled. "It's coming for us!"

He caught a glimpse of a figure up ahead of him, then of Wendell's face, smeared by the mist, turning to say:

"There's no way out!"

"There has to be!"

"I can't find it!" Wendell said, his reply almost drowned out by the din of Carna's shrieks.

Harvey glanced back the way he'd come, more afraid not to know how close the creature was than to see it, however terrifying the sight. A veil of mist swirled in front of him, but he glimpsed Carna's form as the beast descended. It was the most monstrous of the brood: its skin rotted and stretched over barbed and polished bone, its throat a nest of snaky tongues, its jaws set with hundreds of teeth.

This is the end, Harvey thought. I've only been alive ten years and five months and I'm going to have my head bitten off.

Then, from the corner of his eye, a strange sight. Mrs. Griffin's arms, reaching into the mist, and dropping Blue-Cat to the ground.

"He's got a good sense of direction!" Harvey heard her say. "Follow him! Follow him!"

He didn't need a second invitation. Nor did Blue-Cat. Tail up, it padded off, and Harvey hauled on Wendell's arm to drag him in pursuit. The cat was quick, but so was Harvey. He kept his eyes glued on that bright tail, even when the rush of wings behind him announced that Carna had entered the mist and was almost upon them.

Two strides; three strides; four. And now the mist seemed to be thinning. He heard Wendell whooping for joy—"The street!" he yelled, "I see it!"—and the next moment Harvey saw it too, the sidewalks wet with rain and shining in the lamplight.

Now he dared look back, and there was Carna, its jaws a yard from them.

He let go of Wendell's arm and pushed his friend toward the street, ducking as he did so. Carna's lower jaw scraped his spine, but the beast was moving too fast to check itself, and instead of wheeling around to scoop up its quarry it flew on, out into the real world.

Wendell was already there; Harvey joined him a moment later.

"We did it!" Wendell yelled. *"We did it!"*

"So did Carna!" Harvey said, pointing up at the beast as it rose against the cloudy sky and turned to come back for them.

"It wants to drive us back inside!" Harvey said.

"I'm not going!" Wendell cried. "Never! I'm *never* going in there again!"

Carna heard his defiance. Its blazing eyes fixed on him and it came down like a thunderbolt, its shriek echoing through the midnight streets.

"Run!" Harvey said.

But Carna's stare had rooted Wendell to the spot. Harvey grabbed hold of him and was about to make a run for it when he heard the beast's cry change. Triumph became doubt; doubt became pain; and suddenly Carna wasn't swooping but *falling*, holes opening in its wings as though a horde of invisible moths was eating at their fabric.

It labored to climb the air again, but its wounded wings refused their duty, and seconds later it struck the street so hard it bit off a dozen of its tongues, and scattered half a hundred teeth at the boys' feet. The fall didn't kill it, however. Though agonized by its wounds, it hauled itself up onto the spiky crutches of its wings and began to drag itself back toward the wall. Even now, in this wretched state, it was ferocious, and with snaps to right and left drove Harvey and Wendell out of its path.

"It can't survive out here . . ." Wendell realized aloud, ". . . it's dying."

Harvey wished he had some weapon to keep the beast from returning to safety, but he had to be content with the sight of its defeat. If it had not wanted their flesh so badly, he thought, it wouldn't have come after them at such speed, and brought this pain and humiliation upon itself. There was a lesson there, if he could only remember it. Evil, however powerful it seemed, could be undone by its own appetite.

Then the creature was gone, a curtain of mist drawn over its retreat.

There was only one sign remaining of the mysteries that lay on the other side of the wall: the face of Blue-Cat, gazing out at the world that he, like all the occupants of the Holiday House, could never explore. His azure gaze met Harvey's for a moment; then he looked back toward his prison, as though he heard Mrs. Griffin's summons, and with a sorrowful sigh turned and traipsed away.

"Weird," said Wendell, as he stared at the rainy streets. "It's as though I never left."

"Is it?" said Harvey. He wasn't so sure. He felt different; *marked* by this adventure.

"I wonder if we'll even remember we came here in a week's time?"

"Oh, I'll remember," Harvey said. "I've got a few souvenirs."

He dug into his pocket in search of the figures from the ark. Even as he pulled them out he felt them crumbling, as the real world took its toll on them.

"Illusions . . ." he murmured as they turned to dust and ran away between his fingers.

"Who cares?" said Wendell. "It's time to go home. And that's no illusion."

XIV

Time Was

I<small>T TOOK THE BOYS AN HOUR TO REACH THE CENTER OF</small> town, and there—given that their houses lay in opposite directions—they parted company. They exchanged addresses before they did so, promising to contact each other in a day or two, so that they could each support the other's account of the Holiday House. It would be difficult to make people believe all that had happened to them, but perhaps they'd have a better chance if two voices told the same tale.

"I know what you did back there," Wendell said just before they parted. "You saved my life."

"You would have done the same thing for me," Harvey said.

Wendell looked doubtful. "I might have *wanted* to," he said, somewhat abashed, "but I've never been very brave."

"We escaped together," Harvey said. "I couldn't have done it without you."

"Really?"

"Really."

Wendell brightened at this. "Yeah," he said. "I guess that's right. Well . . . be seein' ya."

And, with that, they went their separate ways. It was still several hours before daybreak, and the streets were virtually deserted, so for Harvey it was a long, lonely trudge home. He was tired, and a little saddened by his farewell to Wendell, but the thought of the welcome he'd get when he reached his own doorstep put a spring in his heels.

Several times he wondered if he'd gone astray, because the streets he passed through were unfamiliar. One neighborhood was extremely fancy, the houses and the cars parked outside them slicker than anything he'd set eyes on. Another was virtually a wasteland, the houses half rubble, the streets strewn with garbage. But his sense of direction served him well. As the East began to pale, and the birds in the trees started their twitterings, he rounded the corner of his street. His weary legs broke into a joyful dash, and brought him to the step, panting for breath and ready to fall into his parents' arms.

He knocked on the door. There was no sound from the house at first, which didn't surprise him given the hour. He knocked again, and again. Finally, a light was turned on and he heard somebody coming to the door.

"Who is it?" said his father from behind the closed door. "Do you know what time it is?"

"It's me," said Harvey.

Then came the sound of bolts being drawn aside, and the door was opened a crack.

"Who's *me?*" said the man peering out at him.

He looked kindly enough, Harvey thought, but it wasn't his father. This was a much older man, his hair almost white, his face thin. He had a badly trimmed mustache, and a furrow of a frown.

"What do you want?" he said.

Before Harvey could reply a woman's voice said:

"Come away from the door."

He couldn't see the second speaker yet, but he caught a glimpse of the wallpaper in the hallway, and the pictures on the wall. To his relief he saw that this was not his house at all. He'd obviously made a simple mistake, and knocked on the wrong door.

"I'm sorry," he said, backing away. "I didn't mean to wake you up."

"Who are you looking for?" the man wanted to know, opening the door a little wider now. "Are you one of the Smith kids?"

He started to dig in the pocket of his dressing gown, and brought out a pair of spectacles.

He can't even see me properly, Harvey thought: poor old man.

But before the spectacles reached the bridge of the man's nose his wife appeared behind him, and Harvey's legs almost folded up beneath him at the sight of her.

She was old, this woman, her hair almost as colorless as her husband's, and her face even more lined and sorrowful. But Harvey knew that face better than any on earth. It was the first face he'd ever loved. It was his mother.

"Mom?" he murmured.

The woman stopped and stared out through the open door at the boy standing on the step, her eyes filling up with tears. She could barely breathe the word she said next.

"Harvey?"

"Mom? . . . Mom, it *is* you, isn't it?"

By now the man had put on his spectacles, and peered through them with his eyes wide.

"It's not possible," he said flatly. "This can't be Harvey."

"It's him," said his wife. "It's our Harvey. He's come home."

The man shook his head. "After all these years?" he said. "He'd be a man by now. He'd be a grown man. This is just a boy."

"It's him, I tell you."

"No!" the man replied, angry now. "It's some prank. Somebody trying to break our hearts. As if they're not broken enough."

He started to slam the door, but Harvey's mom caught hold of it.

"Look at him," she said. "Look at his clothes. That's what he was wearing the night he left us."

"How do you know?"

"You think I don't remember?"

"It's *thirty-one years ago,*" said Harvey's father, still staring at the boy on the step. "This can't . . . can't be . . ." He faltered as slow recognition spread over his face. "Oh my Lord," he said, his voice dropping to a hoarse whisper, ". . . it *is* him, isn't it?"

"I told you," his wife replied.

"Are you some kind of *ghost?*" he asked Harvey.

"Oh for goodness' sake," Harvey's mom said. "He's no ghost!" She slipped past her husband, and out onto the step. "I don't know how it's possible, and I don't care," she said, opening her arms to Harvey. "All I know is, our little boy's come home to us."

Harvey couldn't speak. There were too many tears in his throat, and in his nose and in his eyes. All he could do was stumble into his mother's arms. It was wonderful to feel her hands stroke his hair and her fingers wipe his cheeks.

"Oh Harvey, Harvey, Harvey," she sobbed. "We thought we'd never see you again." She kissed him over and over. "We thought you'd gone forever."

"How's this *possible?*" his father still wanted to know.

"I kept praying," his mother said.

Harvey had another answer, though he didn't voice it. The moment he'd set eyes on his mother—so changed, so sorrowful—it was instantly clear what a terrible trick Hood's House had played upon them all. For every day he'd spent there a year had gone by here in the real world. Every morning while he'd played in the spring warmth, months had passed. In the afternoon, while he'd lazed in the summer sun, the same. And those haunted twilights, which had seemed so brief, had been another span of months, as had the Christmas nights, full of snow and presents. They'd all slipped by so easily, and though *he* had only aged a month, his mom and dad had lived in sadness for thirty-one years, thinking that their little boy had gone forever.

That had almost been the case. If he'd remained in the House of Illusions, distracted by its petty pleasures, a whole lifetime would have gone by here in the real world, and his soul would have become Hood's property. He would have joined the fish circling in the lake; and circling; and circling. He shuddered at the thought.

"You're cold, sweetie," his mother said. "Let's get you inside."

He sniffed hard, and cleared his tears with the back of his hand.

"I'm so tired," he said.

"I'll make a bed for you straight away."

"No, I want to tell you what happened before I go to sleep," Harvey replied. "It's a long story. Thirty-one years long."

XV

New Nightmares

It was a more difficult tale to tell than he expected it to be. Though some of the details were clear in his head—Rictus's first appearance; the sinking of the ark; his and Wendell's escape—there was much else he could not properly remember. It was as though the mist he'd strode through had seeped into his head, and had there drawn a veil over the House and much of what it contained.

"I remember speaking to you on the phone two or three times," he said.

"You didn't speak to us, honey," his mom replied.

"Then that was just another trick," Harvey said. "I should have known."

"But who was *playing* all those tricks?" his father demanded. "If this House exists—I say *if*—then whoever owns it kidnapped you and somehow kept you from growing up. Maybe he *froze* you—"

"No," said Harvey. "It was warm there, except when the snow came down, of course."

"There has to be *some* sane explanation."

"There *is*," said Harvey. "It was magic."

His father shook his head. "That's a child's answer," he said. "And I'm not a child anymore."

"And I know what I know," said Harvey firmly.

"It isn't very much, honey," his mom said.

"I wish I could remember more."

She put a comforting arm around his shoulder. "Never mind," she said, "we'll talk about it when you've had a rest."

"Could you find this House again?" his father asked him.

"Yes," Harvey replied, though his skin ran with chills at the thought of going back. "I think so."

"Then that's what we'll do."

"I don't want him going back to that place," his mother said.

"We have to know it exists before we report it to the police. You understand that, don't you, son?"

Harvey nodded. "It sounds like something I made up, I know. But it's not. I swear it's not."

"Come on, sweetie," his mother said. "I'm afraid your room's changed a bit, but it's still comfortable. I kept it just as you'd left it for years and years, hoping you'd find your way home. Then I realized if you ever *did* come back you'd be a grown man, and you wouldn't want it decorated with rocket ships and parrots. So we had the decorators in. It's completely different now."

"I don't mind," Harvey said. "It's home, and that's all I care about."

IN THE EARLY AFTERNOON, AS HE SLEPT IN HIS OLD ROOM, it rained: a hard March rain that beat against the window and slapped on the sill. The sound woke him. He sat up in bed with the hairs at his nape pricking and knew that he'd been dreaming of Lulu. Poor, lost Lulu, dragging her misshapen body through the bushes, her flipper hand clutching the ark animals she'd dredged up from the mud.

The thought of her unhappiness was unbearable. How could he ever hope to live in the world to which he'd returned, knowing that she remained Hood's prisoner?

"I'll find you," he murmured to himself. "I will, I swear..."

Then he lay back on the cold pillow, and listened to the sound of rain until sleep crept over him.

Exhausted by his travels and traumas, he didn't wake

again until the following morning. The rain had cleared. It was time to lay plans.

"I bought a map of the whole of Millsap," his father said, unfolding his purchase and spreading it over the kitchen table. "There's our house." He had already marked the place with a cross. "Now, do you remember any of the street names around Hood's place?"

Harvey shook his head. "I was too busy escaping," he said.

"Were there any particular buildings you saw?"

"It was dark, and rainy."

"So we just have to trust to luck."

"We'll find it," Harvey said. "Even if it takes all week."

IT WAS EASIER SAID THAN DONE. MORE THAN THREE DE-cades had passed since he'd first made his way through the town with Rictus, and countless things had changed. There were new plazas and new slums; new cars on the streets and new aircraft overhead. So many distractions, all keeping Harvey from the trail.

"I don't know which way is which," he admitted, after they'd been searching for half a day. "Nothing's the way I remember it."

"We'll keep going," his father said. "It'll all come clear."

It didn't. They spent the rest of the day wandering around, hoping that some sight would trigger a memory, but it was a frustrating business. Every now and then, in some square or street, Harvey would say: "Maybe this is it," and they'd head off in one direction or another, only to find that the trail grew cold a few blocks on.

That evening, his father quizzed him again.

"If you could only remember what the House *looked* like," he said, "I could describe it to people."

"It was big, I remember that. And old. I'm sure it was very old."

"Could you draw it?"

"I could try."

He did just that, and though he wasn't much of an artist his hand seemed to remember more than his brain had, because after a half hour he had drawn the House in considerable detail. His father was pleased.

"We'll take this with us tomorrow," he said. "Maybe somebody will recognize it."

But the second day was just as frustrating as the first. Nobody knew the House that Harvey had drawn, nor anything remotely like it. By the end of the afternoon, Harvey's father was getting short-tempered.

"It's useless!" he said. "I must have asked five hundred people and not one of them—*not one*—even vaguely recognized the place."

"It's not surprising," said Harvey. "I don't think anyone who saw the House—besides me and Wendell—ever escaped before."

"We should just repeat all this to the police," his mother said, "and let them deal with it."

"And what do we tell them?" his father said, raising his voice. "That we *think* there's a House out there that hides in a mist, and steals children with *magic*? It's ridiculous!"

"Calm down, calm down," Harvey's mother said. "We'll talk about this after we've eaten."

They trudged home, ate and discussed the whole problem again, but without finding any solutions. Mr. Hood had laid his traps carefully over the years, protecting himself from the laws of the real world. Safe behind the mists of his illusion, he'd most likely already found two new and unwitting prisoners to replace Harvey and Wendell. It seemed his evil would go on, undiscovered and unpunished.

The following day Harvey's father made an announcement.

"This search is getting us nowhere," he said. "We're going to give it up."

"Are you going to the police?" his wife asked him.

"Yes. And they'll want Harvey to tell them everything he knows. It's going to be difficult, son."

"They won't believe me," Harvey said.

"That's why I'm going to talk to them first," his father said. "I'll find somebody who'll listen."

He left soon after breakfast, with a worried expression on his face.

"This is all my fault," Harvey said to his mom. "We lost all that time together, just because I was *bored*."

"Don't blame yourself," she said. "We're all tempted to do things we regret once in a while. Sometimes we choose badly and make mistakes."

"I just wish I knew how to *un*make it," Harvey replied.

His mother went out shopping in the middle of the morning, and left Harvey haunted by that thought. Was there some way to undo the damage that had been done? To take back the stolen years, and live them here, with the people who loved him, and whom he loved dearly in return?

He was sitting at his bedroom window, trying to puzzle the problem out, when he saw a forlorn figure at the street corner. He threw open the window and yelled down to him:

"Wendell! Wendell! Over here!"

Then he raced downstairs. By the time he opened the door his friend was on the step, his face red and wet with tears and sweat.

"What happened?" he said. "Everything's changed." His words were punctuated by hiccups. "My dad divorced my mom and my mom's so *old,* Harvey, and fat as a house." He wiped his running nose with the back of his hand, and sniffed hard. "It wasn't supposed to be this way!" he said. "Well, was it?"

Harvey did his best to explain how the House had deceived them, but Wendell was in no mood for theory. He just wanted the nightmare to be over.

"I want things the way they were," he wailed.

"My dad's gone to the police," Harvey said. "He's going to tell them everything."

"That won't do any good," Wendell said despairingly. "They'll never find the House."

"You're right," Harvey said. "I went to look for it with my mom and dad, but it was no use. It's hiding."

"Well it's bound to hide from *them,* stupid," Wendell said. "It doesn't want grown-ups."

"You're right," said Harvey. "It wants children. And I bet it wants you and me more than ever."

"How'd you reckon that?"

"It almost had us. It almost ate us alive."

"So you think it's got a taste for us?"

"I'm sure of it."

Wendell stared at his feet for a moment. "You think we should go back, don't you?"

"I don't think any of those grown-ups—my dad, your mom, the police—are *ever* going to find the House. If we want all those years back, we have to get them for ourselves."

"I don't much like the idea," Wendell confessed.

"Neither do I," he said, thinking as he spoke that he'd have to leave a note for his mom and dad, so that they wouldn't think his return had been a dream. "We have to go," he said. "We don't have any choice."

"So when do we start?"

"Now!" said Harvey grimly. "We've lost too much time already."

XVI

Back to the Happy Land

IT WAS AS IF THE HOUSE KNEW THAT THEY WERE COM-
ing back and was calling to them. As soon as they stepped out
into the street their feet seemed to know the way. All they had
to do was let them lead.

"What do we do when we get there?" Wendell wanted to
know. "I mean, we only just escaped with our lives last time—"

"Mrs. Griffin will help us," Harvey said.

Wendell's breath quickened. "Suppose Carna bit her head
off?" he said.

"Then we'll have to do it alone."

"Do what?"

"Find Hood."

"But you told me he was dead."

"I don't think being dead means much to a creature like
him," Harvey said. "He's in the house somewhere, Wendell,
and we have to hunt him down whether we like it or not. He's
the one who stole all those years with our moms and dads. And
we won't get them back until we face him."

"You make it sound easy," Wendell said.

"The whole House is a box of tricks," Harvey reminded
him. "The seasons. The presents. They're all illusions. We have
to hold on to that."

"Harvey? Look."

Wendell pointed ahead of them. Harvey knew the street
at a glance. Thirty-three days ago, he'd stood here with Rictus,
and listened to the tempter tell him what a fine place lay on the
other side of the mist wall up ahead.

"This is it then," Harvey said.

It was strange, but he didn't feel afraid, even though he knew they were walking back into their enemy's arms. It was better to face Hood and his illusions now than to spend the rest of his life wondering about Lulu, and mourning the years he'd lost.

"Are you ready?" he asked Wendell.

"Before we go," his friend replied, "can we get just one thing straight? If the House *is* all illusions, then how come we felt the cold? And how come I got fat from eating Mrs. Griffin's pies, and—"

"I don't know," Harvey cut in, doubt running a cold finger up his spine. "I can't explain how Hood's magic works. All I know is, he took all those years away to feed himself."

"Feed?"

"Yeah. Like . . . like . . . like a *vampire*."

This was the first time Harvey had thought of Hood that way, but it instinctively seemed right. Blood was life, and life was what Hood fed upon. He was a vampire, sure enough. Maybe a king among vampires.

"So shouldn't we have a stake, or holy water, or something?"

"That's just in stories," Harvey said.

"But if he comes after us—"

"We fight."

"Fight with what?"

Harvey shrugged. The truth was, he didn't know. But he was sure that crosses and prayers weren't going to be any use in the battle that lay ahead.

"No more talk," he said to Wendell. "If you don't want to come, then don't."

"I didn't say that."

"Good," said Harvey, and started toward the mist.

Wendell followed on his heels, and just as Harvey stepped

into the wall he snatched hold of his friend's sleeve, so that they entered as they had exited: together.

The mist closed around them like a waterlogged blanket, pressing so hard against their faces Harvey half thought it intended to smother them. But it only wished to keep them from changing their minds. A moment later a tremor moved through its folds and spat them out the other side.

It was high summer in Hood's kingdom: the lazy season. The sun, which had been hidden by rain clouds on the other side of the mist, was beaming down on the House and all that prospered around it. The trees swayed in a balmy breeze, the doors and windows of the House, its porch and chimneys, all gleamed as if newly painted.

There were welcoming songs in the eaves; welcoming smells from the kitchen; welcoming laughter through the open door. Welcome; everywhere welcome.

"I'd forgotten . . ." Wendell murmured.

"Forgotten what?"

"How . . . *beautiful* it is."

"Don't trust it," Harvey said. "It's all illusion, remember? All of it."

Wendell didn't reply, but wandered away toward the trees. The honeyed breeze gusted around him, as if to pluck him up. He didn't resist, but went where it led, into the dappled shade.

"Wendell!" Harvey said, following him across the lawn. "We've got to stick together."

"I'd forgotten about the tree house," Wendell said dreamily, staring up into the canopy. "We had such fun up there, remember?"

"No," said Harvey, determined not to let the past distract him from his mission here. "I don't remember."

"Yes, you do," said Wendell, smiling from ear to ear. "We worked so hard up there. I'm going up to see how it looks."

Harvey grabbed his arm.

"No you're not."

"Yes I *am,*" he snapped back, wrenching his arm from Harvey's grip. "I can do whatever I want. You don't *own* me."

Harvey could see by the glazed look in Wendell's eyes that the House was already working its seductive magic. It could only be a matter of time, he knew, before his own powers of resistance were worn away. And what then? Would he forget his work here entirely, and become an empty-headed boy, laughing like a loon while his soul was sucked away?

"No!" he said aloud, *"I'm not going to let you do it!"*

"Do what?" said Wendell.

"We've got work to do!" Harvey told him.

"Who cares?" Wendell replied.

"I do. And so did you five minutes ago. Remember what it did to us, Wendell."

The wind in the trees seemed to sigh at this.

"Aaahh . . ." it said, as if it now understood Harvey's purpose here, and would waft this intelligence to the ears of Mr. Hood.

Harvey didn't care. In fact, he was pleased.

"Go on," he said, as the gusts flew toward the House. "Tell him! Tell him!" He turned on Wendell. "Are you coming?" he said. "Or am I going to go in alone?"

"I don't mind going in," Wendell said cheerily. "I'm hungry."

Harvey stared hard at Wendell. "Don't you remember *anything* we said out there?" he demanded.

"Of course I do," Wendell replied. "We said we were going to . . ." He paused, frowning. ". . . going . . . to . . ."

"This place has stolen time that belonged to us, Wendell."

"How did it do that?" said Wendell, still frowning deeply. "It's just . . . just . . ." Again he faltered, searching for the words. ". . . just such a *perfect* day." The frown began to fade again, and a broad smile replaced it. "Who cares?" Wendell said. "I mean, on a day like this, *who cares?* Let's just enjoy ourselves."

Harvey shook his head. He was losing precious time here, which was exactly what Hood and the House wanted. Instead of wasting any further words on Wendell, he turned on his heel and headed toward the front door.

"Wait for me!" Wendell hollered. "Can you smell that pie?"

Harvey could, and wished he'd put some food in his belly before he'd started out on this adventure. Knowing that these tantalizing smells were all part of Hood's repertoire wasn't enough to stop his mouth from watering or his stomach from grumbling.

All he could do was think of the dust to which his ark animals had turned when he'd stepped out into the street. The pie on the kitchen table was probably made of the same bitter stuff, concealed beneath a veneer of sweetness. He held on to that thought as best he could, knowing that the House into which he was about to step would be full of such blandishments.

With Wendell again trailing a step behind, he climbed the porch steps and marched into the House. The moment they were both inside, the door slammed behind them. Harvey reeled around, his skin crawling. It was not the wind that had thrown the door shut.

It was Rictus.

XVII

Cook, Cat and Coffin

GREAT TO HAVE YOU BACK, BOY," RICTUS SAID, HIS smile as wide as ever. "I told everyone you wouldn't be able to stay away. Nobody believed me. *He's gone,* they said, *he's gone.* But I knew better." He started to wander toward Harvey. "I knew you wouldn't be satisfied with a little visit . . . not with so much *fun* still to be had."

"I'm hungry," Wendell whined.

"Help yourselves!" Rictus grinned.

Wendell was off at a sprint, into the kitchen.

"Oh boy oh boy oh boy!" he hollered. "Look at all this *food.*"

Harvey didn't reply.

"Aren't you hungry?" Rictus said, raising an eyebrow high above his spectacles. He cupped his hand behind his ear. "That sounds like an empty belly to me."

"Where's Mrs. Griffin?" Harvey said.

"Oh . . . she's around," Rictus said mischievously. "But she's getting old. She takes to her bed a good deal these days, so we laid her down somewhere safe and sound."

As he spoke there was a mewling sound from the living room, and there at the door stood Stew-Cat. Rictus scowled. "Get out of here, pussy!" he spat. "Can't you see we're having a conversation?"

But Stew-Cat wasn't about to be intimidated. She sauntered over to Harvey, rubbing herself against his legs.

"What do you want?" Harvey said, going down on his haunches to stroke her. She purred loudly.

"Hey, that's fine and dandy," Rictus said, putting off his

anger in favor of a freshly polished smile. "You like the cat. The cat likes you. Everybody's happy."

"I'm not happy," Harvey said.

"And why's that?"

"I left all my presents here, and I don't know where."

"No problem," said Rictus. "I'll find 'em for you."

"Would you do that?" Harvey said.

"Sure, kid," said Rictus, persuaded that his charm was working again. "That's what we're all here for: to give you whatever your heart desires."

"I think maybe I left them up in my bedroom," Harvey suggested.

"You know I think I saw 'em up there," Rictus replied. "You stay *right here*. I'll be back."

He took himself up the stairs two and three at a time, whistling tunelessly through his teeth as he ascended. Harvey waited until he disappeared from sight and then went to check on Wendell, letting Stew-Cat slip away.

"Ah, now, look at this!" a voice said as he appeared at the kitchen door.

It was Jive. He was standing at the stove, as sinewy as ever, juggling eggs with one hand and tossing pancakes in a pan with the other.

"What do you fancy?" he said. "Sweet or savory?"

"Nothing," Harvey said.

"It's all good," Wendell piped up. He was almost hidden behind a wall of filled plates. "Try the apple turnovers! They're great!"

Harvey was sorely tempted. The buffet looked wonderfully tempting. But it was dust. He *had* to keep remembering that.

"Maybe later," he said, averting his eyes from the heaps of syrup-drenched waffles and bowls of ice cream.

"Where are you going?" Jive wanted to know.

"Mr. Rictus is finding a few presents for me," Harvey said.

Jive smiled with satisfaction. "So you're getting back into the swing of things, kiddo!" he said. "Good for you!"

"I've missed being here," Harvey replied.

He didn't linger, just in case Jive saw the lie in his eyes, but turned and headed back into the hallway. Stew-Cat was still there, staring at him.

"What is it?" he said.

The cat took off toward the stairs, then stopped and cast a backward glance.

"Have you something to show me?" Harvey whispered.

At this, the cat bounded off again. Harvey followed, expecting her to lead the way upstairs. But before she reached the bottom step she veered off to her left, and led Harvey down a narrow passage to a door he had never even noticed before.

He rattled the handle, but the door was locked. Turning to look for Stew-Cat, he found her rubbing her arched back against the leg of a small table set nearby. On the table was a carved wooden box. In the box was a key.

He went back to the door, unlocked it, and pulled it open. There was a flight of wooden steps in front of him, leading down into a darkness from which a sour, dank smell rose. He might have declined to descend had Stew-Cat not hurried on past him, down into the murk.

With his fingers trailing on the damp walls to the left and right of him, he followed Stew-Cat to the bottom of the flight, counting the steps as he went. There were fifty-two, and by the time he had descended them all his eyes had become reasonably accustomed to the gloom. The cellar was cavernous but empty, except for a litter of rubble and a large wooden box, which lay in the dust maybe a dozen yards from where he stood.

"What is it?" he hissed to Stew-Cat, knowing the creature had no way of replying, but hoping for some sign nevertheless.

Stew-Cat's only answer was to run across the floor and leap nimbly up onto the box, where it began to claw at the wood.

Harvey's curiosity was stronger than his fear, but not so much stronger that he dashed to pull off the lid. He approached as though the box were some sleeping beast, which for all he knew it was. The closer he got the more it resembled a crude coffin; but what kind of coffin was sealed with a padlock? Was this where Carna had been laid, perhaps, after the beast had dragged its wounded body back home? Was it even now listening to Stew-Cat scratch on the lid, waiting for release?

As he came within a yard of the casket, however, he laid eyes on a clue to its contents: an apron string, left hanging out of the box by whoever had locked it. He knew of only one person in the House who wore an apron.

"Mrs. Griffin!" he whispered, digging his fingernails under the lid. "Mrs. Griffin? Are you in there?"

There was a muffled thump from inside.

"I'm going to get you out," he promised, hauling on the lid as hard as he could.

He didn't have the strength to break the lock. In desperation he began to search the cellar, looking for some tool or other, and found himself two sizable rocks. Hefting them, he returned to the casket.

"This is going to be noisy," he warned Mrs. Griffin.

Then, using one stone as a kind of chisel and the other as a hammer, he assaulted the lock. Blue sparks flew as he struck at the metal, but he seemed to be making no impression until, all of a sudden, the lock gave a loud crack and fell to the ground.

He paused for a moment, a feather of doubt brushing his brow. Suppose it *was* Carna's coffin? Then he threw the rocks aside and hauled off the lid.

XVIII

The Bitter Truth

H<small>E ALMOST SHOUTED OUT LOUD, SEEING THE TERRI-</small>ble state that poor Mrs. Griffin was in. She was staring up at him with wild eyes, her hair pulled out in clawfuls, her face purple with bruises. A foul rag had been stuffed into her mouth. Harvey carefully removed it, and she began to speak, her voice a hoarse whisper.

"Thank you, my sweet, thank you," she said. "But oh, you shouldn't have come back. It's too dangerous here."

"Who did this to you?"

"Jive and Rictus."

"But *he* ordered it, didn't he?" Harvey said, helping her up. "Don't tell me he's dead, because I know that doesn't matter. Hood's here in the House, isn't he?"

"Yes," she said, holding on to him as she climbed up out of the box. "Yes, he's here. But not in the way you think . . ." She began to weep, the tears clogging her words.

"It's all right," Harvey said. "Everything's going to be all right."

Her fingers went up to her face, and touched the tears. "I thought . . . I thought I'd never cry again," she said. "Look what you've done!"

"I'm sorry," said Harvey.

"Oh no, my sweet, don't be sorry. It's *wonderful*." She smiled through her tears. "You've broken his curse on me."

"What curse?"

"Oh, it's a long story."

"I want to hear."

"I was the first child who ever came to Hood's House," she

said. "This was many, many years ago. I was nine when I first walked up the front path. I'd run away from home, you see."

"Why?"

"My cat had died and my father refused to buy me another. And what do you think Rictus gave me the very day I arrived?"

"Three cats," said Harvey.

"You know how this House works, don't you?"

Harvey nodded. "It gives you whatever you think you want."

"And I wanted cats, and a home, and—"

"What?"

"Another father." She shivered with fear, remembering the horror. "I met Hood that night. At least, I heard his voice."

Stew-Cat had come to her feet, and she paused to stoop and gather the creature into her arms.

"Where did you hear him?" Harvey asked.

"In the attic at the top of the House. And he said to me: *If you stay here, forever and ever, you'll never die.* You'll grow old, but you'll live until the end of time, and never weep again."

"And that's what you wanted?"

"It was stupid, but yes, I did. I was afraid, you see. Afraid of being put into the ground like my cat." A new wave of tears came, running down her pale cheeks. "I was running away from Death—"

"—straight into its House," Harvey said.

"Oh no, child," Mrs. Griffin said. "Hood isn't Death." She wiped away her tears, so as to see Harvey more clearly. "Death is a natural thing. Hood isn't. I would welcome Death now, like a friend I'd driven away from my door. I've seen too much, my sweet. Too many seasons, too many children . . ."

"Why didn't you try and stop him?"

"I have no power against him. All I could do was give the children who came here as much happiness as I knew how."

"So how old are you?" Harvey asked her.

"Who knows?" she replied, laying her cheek against Stew-Cat's fur. "I grew up and old in a matter of days, but then the passage of time seemed to lose its hold on me. Sometimes I've wanted to ask one of the children: *What year is it in the world outside?*"

"I can tell you."

"Don't," she said, putting her finger to her lips. "I don't want to know how the years have flown. It would hurt too much."

"What *do* you want, then?"

"To die," she said, with a little smile. "To slip out of this skin, and go to the stars."

"Is that what happens?"

"It's what I believe," she said. "But Hood won't let me die. Not ever. That'll be his revenge on me, for helping you to escape. He already had Blue-Cat murdered, for showing you the way out."

"Hood's going to let you go," Harvey said. "I promise. I'm going to make him."

She shook her head. "You're so brave, my sweet," she said. "But he won't let any of us go. There's such a terrible emptiness inside him. He wants to fill it with souls, but it's a pit. A bottomless pit—"

"—and you're both heading for it," said an oily voice. The speaker was Marr. She was oozing down the stairs. "We've been looking for you up and down," she said to Harvey. "You'd better come with me, child."

She extended her arms in Harvey's direction. He remembered all too well her transforming touch. "Come! Come!" she said. "I might still get you out of trouble, if you let me make something *humble* of you. He likes humble things, does Mr. Hood. Fleas; worms; scabby dogs. Come to me, child! *Quickly!*"

Harvey looked around the cellar. There were no other

ways out. If he was to get Mrs. Griffin up into the sun it had to be by way of the stairs, and Marr was standing in front of them.

He took a step in her direction. She smiled toothlessly.

"Good, child, good," she said.

"Don't," Mrs. Griffin said. "She'll hurt you."

"*Hush,* woman!" Marr said. "We're going to have to *nail* that lid down next time!" Her greasy green eyes swiveled back in Harvey's direction. "*He* knows what's good for him. Don't you, boy?"

Harvey didn't reply. He simply kept walking toward Marr, whose fingers seemed to be growing like a snail's horns, reaching out to fix upon his face.

"You've been such an *obedient* boy," Marr went on. "Maybe I won't turn you into a worm after all. What would you like to be? Tell me. Tell me what's in your heart . . ."

"Never mind *my* heart," Harvey said, reaching out toward Marr. "What about *yours?*"

A puzzled look came over Marr's face. "Mine?" she said.

"Yes," said Harvey. "What do *you* dream of being?"

"I never dream," she said defiantly.

"You should try it," Harvey told her. "If you can change me into a worm, or a bat, what could you do for *yourself?*"

The defiance on her face became bafflement, and the bafflement turned to panic. Her outstretched fingers began to retreat into themselves. Harvey reached for them like lightning, however, interweaving his fingers with hers.

"What do you want to be?" he said to her. "*Think!*"

She started to struggle, and he felt her magic surging through her fingers into his, attempting to work some change on him. But he didn't want to be a vampire bat anymore, and he certainly didn't want to be a worm. He was quite happy to be himself. The magic therefore had no hold on him; instead it flowed back into Marr, who began to shake as though she were being dipped in icy water.

"What . . . are . . . you . . . *doing?*" she demanded.

"Tell me what's in your heart," he said, returning her invitation.

"I'm not telling *you!*" she replied, still trying to wrest her fingers free of his.

But she was not used to having her victims resist her this way. Her muscles were soft and flabby. She pulled and pulled, but she couldn't escape him.

"Leave me alone!" she said. "If you harm me Mr. Hood will have your head."

"I'm not harming you," Harvey replied. "I'm just letting you have your dreams, the way you let me have mine."

"*I don't want them!*" she yelled, struggling more than ever.

He wouldn't let her go. Instead, he drew closer to her, as if to wrap her up in his arms. She started to spit at him—great gobs of slime—but he wiped them from his face and kept approaching her.

"No . . ." she began to murmur, ". . . no . . ."

But she couldn't keep the magic she'd intended for him from working on her own skin and bones. Her fat face began to soften and run like melting wax; her body sagged in its ragged coat, and a greenish gruel began to pour out onto the floor.

"Oh . . ." she sobbed, ". . . you *damnable* child . . ."

What dream was this, Harvey wondered, that was turning Marr to mush? She was growing smaller all the time, her clothes dropping off her as her body shrank, her voice becoming thin. It could only be moments before she disappeared altogether.

"What *do* you dream about?" Harvey said, as Marr's fingers ran away between his own like brackish water.

"I dream of *nothing* . . ." Marr replied, her eyes sinking back into her disintegrating skull, ". . . and that's . . . what . . . I've . . . become . . ." She was almost lost in the folds of her clothes. ". . . nothing . . ." she said again. She was no more than a dirty puddle now; a puddle with a fading voice. ". . . nothing . . ."

Then she was gone, devoured by her own magic.

"You did it!" Mrs. Griffin said. "Child, you did it!"

"One down, three to go," Harvey said.

"Three?"

"Rictus, Jive and Hood himself."

"You're forgetting Carna."

"Is it still alive?"

Mrs. Griffin nodded. "I'm afraid I've heard its shrieks every night. It wants revenge."

"And I want my life back," Harvey said, taking her by the arm and escorting her (still carrying Stew-Cat) to the bottom of the stairs. "I'm going to get it, Mrs. Griffin. Whatever it takes, I'm going to get it."

Mrs. Griffin glanced back at the heap of clothes that marked the place where Marr had vanished into thin air.

"Maybe you can," she said, with astonishment in her voice. "Of all the children who've come here, maybe you're the one who can beat Hood at his own game."

XIX

Dust to Dust

Rictus was waiting at the top of the stairs. His smile was sweet. His words were not.

"You're a murderer now, my little man," he said. "Do you like the feel of Marr's blood on your hands?"

"He didn't kill her," Mrs. Griffin said. "She was never alive. None of you are."

"What are we then?" Rictus asked.

"Illusions," Harvey replied, ushering Mrs. Griffin and her cat past Rictus to the front door. "It's all illusions."

Rictus followed them, giggling insanely.

"What's so funny?" Harvey said, opening the door to let Mrs. Griffin out into the sun.

"You are!" Rictus replied. "You think you know everything, but you don't know Mr. Hood."

"I will in a little while," said Harvey. "Go and get warm," he told Mrs. Griffin. "I'll be back."

"Be careful, child," she said.

"I will," he told her, then closed the door.

"You're a strange one," Rictus said, his smile failing a little. His face, when his teeth no longer dazzled, was like a mask made of dough. Two thumb-holes for eyes, and a blob for a nose.

"I could suck out your brains through your ears," he said, all the music gone from his voice.

"Maybe you could," said Harvey. "But you're not going to."

"How do you know?"

"Because I've got an appointment with your master."

He started toward the bottom of the stairs, but before he

reached it a dark figure flitted in front of him. It was Jive, and he was carrying a plate of apple pie and ice cream.

"It's a long climb," he said. "Put something in your stomach first."

Harvey looked down at the plate. The pie was golden brown and dusted with sugar, the ice cream melting in a sweet, white pool. It certainly looked tempting.

"Go on," said Jive. "You deserve a treat."

"No thanks," Harvey told him.

"Why not?" Jive wanted to know, turning full circle on his heel. "It's lighter than I am."

"But I know what it's made of," Harvey said.

"Apples and cinnamon and—"

"No," said Harvey. "I know what it's *really* made of."

He looked back at the pie, and for a moment it seemed he glimpsed the truth of the thing: the gray dust and ashes from which this illusion was made.

"You think it's poisoned?" Jive said. "Is that it?"

"Maybe," Harvey replied, still staring at the pie.

"Well, it's not!" Jive said. "And I'll prove it!"

Harvey heard Rictus make a warning sound behind him, but Jive didn't catch it. He plunged his fingers into the pie and ice cream and delivered them to his mouth in one swift motion. As he closed his mouth Rictus said: "Don't swallow it!"

Again, too late. The food went down in one gulp. An instant later, Jive dropped the plate and began to slam his fists against his stomach, as if to force the food up again. But instead of half-chewed pie, a cloud of dust issued from between his teeth. Then another; then another.

Half-blinded, Jive snatched at Harvey's throat.

"What . . . have . . . you . . . done?" he coughed.

Harvey had no difficulty shaking himself free.

"It's all dust," he said. "Dirt and dust and ashes! All the food! All the presents! Everything!"

"Help me!" Jive said, clawing at his mouth. "Somebody help me!"

"There's no help for you now!" came a solemn voice.

Harvey looked around. It was Rictus who had spoken, and he was retreating across the hallway, his hands clamped to his face. He stared at Jive between his fingers, his teeth chattering as he voiced the horrid truth. "You shouldn't have eaten that pie," he said. "It's reminding your belly of what you're made of."

"What's that?" Jive said.

"What the boy says," Rictus replied. "Dirt and ashes!"

Jive threw back his head, howling *Noooo!* at this, but even as he opened his mouth to deny it the truth came pouring forth: dry streams of dust that ran from his gullet and flowed over his fingers. It was like a fatal message being passed from one part of his body to another. Touched by the dust his fingers began to crumble in their turn, and as they dropped, the same whisper of decay spread to his thighs and knees and feet.

He started to drop to the ground, but with a final pirouette, swung himself around and grabbed hold of the banister.

"Save me!" he yelled up the stairs. "Mr. Hood, can you hear me? *Please! Please, save me!*"

His legs crumbled beneath him now, but he refused to give up. He started to haul himself up the stairs, still yelling for Mr. Hood to heal him. There was no reply from the heights of the House, however, nor any sound now from Rictus. There were only Jive's pleas and wheezings, and the hiss of dust as it ran away down the stairs from the emptying sack of his body.

"What's going on?" Wendell said, appearing from the kitchen with ketchup smeared around his mouth.

He stared at the cloud of dust that hung around the stairs, unable to see the creature at its heart. Harvey was closer to the cloud, however, and so was witness to Jive's last, terrible moments. The dying creature reached up with an almost fingerless hand, still hoping—even as its life drifted away—that its creator would come to save it. Then it sank down upon the stairs, and its last pitiful fragments crumbled.

"Somebody been beating the carpets?" Wendell said, as Jive's dust settled.

"Two down," Harvey murmured to himself.

"What did you say?" Wendell wanted to know.

Before he replied, Harvey glanced around the hallway, looking for Rictus. But Hood's third servant had disappeared. "It doesn't matter," Harvey said. "Are you done eating?"

"Yeah."

"Was the food good?"

Wendell grinned. *"Yeah."*

Harvey shook his head. "What does *that* mean?" Wendell asked.

Harvey was on the verge of saying: It means you can't help me; it means I have to go up and face Mr. Hood on my own. But what was the use? The House had claimed Wendell entirely. He'd be more of a hindrance than a help in the battle ahead. So instead he said: "Mrs. Griffin's outside."

"So we found her?"

"We found her."

"I'll go say hi," Wendell said with a cheery smile.

"Good idea."

Wendell had his hand on the door when he turned and said: "Where will you be?"

But Harvey didn't answer. He'd already climbed past the heap of dust that marked Jive's demise, and was nearing the top of the first flight, on his way to meet the power that lay waiting in the darkness of the attic.

XX

The Thieves Meet

GLIMPSING THE DUSTY TRUTH MASQUERADING AS PIE and ice cream was one thing, but scratching the veneer of deceits that the House had polished to such perfection was quite another. As Harvey climbed the stairs he kept hoping he'd find some little detail in the walls or the carpets that would allow him to get his mind's fingers beneath the lid of this illusion and lift it up to see what charmless thing lay inside. If Marr had been made of stale mud and spittle, and Jive of dust, what was the House itself made of? But it knew its business too well. However hard Harvey stared, he could not pierce its lies. It delighted his senses with warmth and color and the scents of summer; it cooed softly in his ear and played its gentle airs against his face.

Even when he reached the dark landing at the top of the final flight, the House continued to pretend that this was just another innocent game of hide-and-seek, like the countless games it had seen played in its shadow.

There were five doors ahead of him, every one of them ajar a few inches, as if to say: There are no secrets here, not from a boy who wants the truth. Come look! Come see! *If you dare.*

He dared, but not in the way the House had planned. After spending a few moments examining the doors, he ignored all of them, and instead went back down a flight, chose a strong chair from one of the bedrooms, brought it back upstairs, climbed onto it and pushed open the trap door that let onto the attic.

It was hard work hauling himself up, but he knew, when he'd finished and lay panting on the attic floor, that his pursuit of Hood was almost at an end. The Vampire King was near. Who else but a master of illusions would live in a place so bereft of them? The attic was all the House was not: filthy, murky and cobwebbed.

"Where are you?" he said. It was no use thinking he could surprise the enemy. Hood had watched his ascent from the first stair. "Come out," he yelled, "I want to see what a *thief* looks like."

There was no reply at first, but then—from somewhere at the other end of the attic—Harvey heard a low, guttural growl. Not waiting for his eyes to become fully accustomed to the gloom he started toward the utterance, the boards creaking beneath his feet as he went.

Twice he stopped to look up, because a noise somewhere in the darkness overhead caught his attention. Was it a trapped bird, panicking as it flew blindly back and forth? Or roaches, perhaps, massed on the beams above him?

He told himself to put such imaginings out of his head and concentrate on finding Hood. There were enough real reasons to be fearful here without inventing more. Unlike the area around the trap door, this end of the attic served as some kind of storeroom, and his enemy was surely lurking in the maze of rotting pictures and mildewed furniture. In fact, wasn't that a fluttering motion he saw now out of the corner of his eye?

"Hood?" he said, squinting to try and make better sense of the shape in the shadows. "What are you doing hiding up here?"

He took another step forward, and as he did so he realized his error. This wasn't the mysterious Mr. Hood. He *knew* this shape, mangled though it was: the half-rotted wings; the tiny black eyes; the teeth, the endless teeth.

It was Carna!

The creature half rose from its squalid nest, snapping at

Harvey as it did so. He made a stumbling retreat, and might have been seized after three steps had Carna not been so hobbled by its wounds and slowed by the chaos of its surroundings.

It struck out at the piles of detritus to the left and right of it, scattering chairs and overturning boxes; then hauled itself in pained pursuit of its prey. Harvey kept his eyes fixed upon the beast as he backed away, his mind buzzing with questions. Where was Hood? That was the main mystery. Mrs. Griffin had been certain he was up here somewhere, but Harvey had now wandered the attic from end to end, and its only occupant was the creature driving him back toward the exit.

He chanced several glances into the shadows as he retreated in case he'd missed some figure hiding there. It was not a human form his eyes alighted upon, however; it was a globe the size of a tennis ball, glowing as though filled with starlight. It appeared like a bubble from the boards and rose toward the roof. Momentarily forgetting his jeopardy, Harvey watched it as it ascended, joined by another, then a third and a fourth.

Astonished by the sight, he took too little care where he was walking. He stumbled, fell, and ended up sprawled on the hard boards, staring up at the roof through a red haze of pain.

And there above him was Hood, in all his glory.

His face was spread over the entire roof, his features horribly distorted. His eyes were dark pits gouged into the timbers; his nose was flared and flattened grotesquely, like the nose of an enormous bat; his mouth was a lipless slit that was surely ten feet wide, from which issued a voice that was like the creaking of doors and the howling of chimneys and the rattling of windows.

"Child!" he said. *"You have brought pain into my paradise. Shame on you!"*

"What *pain?*" Harvey shouted back. He was shuddering to his marrow, but he knew this was no time to show his fear.

He would deal in illusion, the way the enemy did; pretending courage even if he didn't feel it. "I came to get what was mine, that's all," he said.

Hood sucked one of the gleaming spheres into his mouth. Its light went out instantly.

"*Marr is dead,*" he said. "*Jive is dead. Gone to muck and dust because of you!*"

"They were never alive," Harvey said.

"*Did you not hear their sobs and pleas?*" Hood demanded, the knots in his brow tightening. "*Did you not pity them?*"

"No," Harvey said.

"*Then I will not pity you,*" came the rasping reply. "*I will watch my poor Carna devour you from sole to scalp, and take pleasure in it.*"

Harvey glanced in Carna's direction. The beast had stopped advancing, but was poised to strike, its dripping jaws inches from Harvey's feet. Now that the beast was still, he could clearly see how badly wounded it was, its body as ragged as a moldy rug, its huge head drooping as though every breath was a burden.

As Harvey stared at it he remembered something Mrs. Griffin had told him: "I would welcome Death now," she'd said, "like a friend I'd driven from my door."

Maybe it wasn't a journey to the stars that was awaiting Carna; maybe it was simply a return to the nothingness from which Hood had conjured it. But the creature wanted that gift nevertheless. It was weary and wounded, kept alive not by any will of its own but because Hood demanded its service.

"*Such a pity . . .*" the voice in the roof murmured.

"What is?" Harvey said, looking back at Hood, who had two more of the globes at his lips. "*To lose you this way,*" he went on. "*Can't I persuade you to think again? After all, I've done you no harm. Why not come back and live here peacefully?*"

"You stole thirty years of time with my mom and dad from me!" Harvey said. "If I stay here you'll steal a lot more."

"I only took the days you didn't want," Hood protested. *"The rainy days. The gray days. The days you wished away. Where's the crime in that?"*

"I didn't know what I was losing," Harvey protested.

"Ah," said Hood softly, *"but isn't that always the way of it? Things slip from your fingers and when they're gone you regret it. But gone is gone, Harvey Swick!"*

"No!" Harvey said. "What you stole I can steal back."

At this, a gleam ignited in the twin pits of Hood's eyes.

"You burn bright, Harvey Swick!" he said. *"I've never known a soul that burned as bright as yours."* He frowned as if studying the boy below. *"Now I understand,"* he said.

"Understand what?"

"Why it is you came back."

Harvey began to say: I came for what you took, but Hood was correcting him before he'd uttered two words.

"You came because you knew you'd find a home here," Hood said. *"We're both thieves, Harvey Swick. I take time. You take lives. But in the end we're the same: both Thieves of Always."*

Repulsive as it was to think of himself in any way similar to this monster, there was some corner of Harvey that feared this was true. The thought silenced him.

"Perhaps we needn't be enemies," Hood said. *"Perhaps I should take you under my wing. My west wing."* He laughed mirthlessly at his own joke. *"I can nurture you. Help you better understand the Dark Paths."*

"So I'll end up feeding on children, like you?" Harvey said. "No thanks."

"I think you'd like it, Harvey Swick," Hood said. *"You've got a streak of the vampire in you already."*

There was no denying this. The very word *vampire* reminded him of his Halloween flight; of soaring against a harvest moon with his eyes burning red and his teeth sharp as razors.

"I see you remember," Hood said, catching the flicker of pleasure on Harvey's face.

Harvey instantly put a scowl in its place. "I don't want to stay here," he said. "I just want to get what's mine and leave."

Hood sighed. *"So sad,"* he said. *"So very sad. But if you will have what's yours, have death. Carna?"* The beast raised its pitiful head. *"Devour the boy!"*

Before the wretched beast could shift itself Harvey scrambled to his feet. In the race to the trap door he knew he had little chance of outrunning Carna; but was there perhaps another way of laying the beast low? If he *was* a Thief of Always, as Hood had said, perhaps it was time to prove it. Not with dust, nor with stolen conjurings, but with the power in his own bones.

Carna took a threatening step toward him, but instead of retreating Harvey extended his hand in the creature's direction, as if to pat its decaying head. It hesitated, its expression mellowing into doubt.

"Devour him . . ." the Vampire King growled.

The beast lowered its head, in expectation of punishment from above. But it was Harvey who laid his hand upon it; a gentle touch that sent a shudder through its body. It raised its snout to press itself against Harvey's palm, and as it did so, let out a long, low moan.

There was neither pain in the sound nor complaint. In fact it was almost a moan of gratitude, that for once it not be met with blows or with howls of horror. It turned its eyes up to Harvey's face, and a shudder of pleasure passed through its body. It seemed to know that the motion would prove fatal, because the instant after, it retreated from its comforter and as it did so its shudders multiplied, and its body suddenly flew into a thousand pieces.

Its teeth, which had seemed so fearsome moments before, rolled away into the darkness; its massive skull shattered; its spine collapsed. In a matter of seconds it was no more than a heap of bone shards, so dry and so aged even the most desperate dog would have passed them by.

Harvey glanced up at the face in the roof. Hood's expression was one of utter perplexity. His mouth was agape, his eyes staring from their pits.

Harvey didn't wait for him to break his silence. He simply turned his back on Carna's remains and hurried toward the trap door, half expecting the creature in the roof to slam it shut. There was no response from Hood, however, until Harvey was lowering himself down onto the chair on the landing. Only then, as Harvey took one last look up at the attic, did Hood speak.

"Oh my little thief . . ." he murmured. *"What shall we do with you now?"*

XXI

Tricks and Temptations

Y OU'VE DONE WELL," SAID THE SMILING FACE AWAIT-
ing him at the top of the stairs.

"I wondered where you'd gone to," Harvey said to Rictus.

"Always ready to serve," came the unctuous reply.

"Really?" said Harvey, stepping down off the chair and approaching the creature.

"Of course," said Rictus. *"Always."*

Now that he was closer to the man, Harvey saw the cracks in his veneer. He was plastering on a smile, and smothering his words in butter and honey, but it was the sour smell of fear that oozed from his sickly skin.

"You're afraid of me, aren't you?" Harvey said.

"No, no," Rictus insisted, "I'm *respectful,* that's all. Mr. Hood thinks you're a bright boy. He's instructed me to offer whatever you want to make you stay." He spread his arms. "The sky's the limit."

"You know what I want."

"Anything but the *years,* thief. You can't have those. You won't even need them if you stay and become Mr. Hood's apprentice. You'll live forever, just like him." He dabbed at the sweat beads on his upper lip with a yellowed handkerchief. "Think about it," he said. "You might be able to kill the likes of Carna . . . or me . . . but you'll never hurt Hood. He's too old; too wise; too *dead.*"

"If I stayed . . ." Harvey said.

Rictus's grin spread. "Yes?" he purred.

"Would the children in the lake go free?"

"Why bother about them?"

"Because one of them was my friend," Harvey reminded him.

"You're thinking of little Lulu, aren't you?" Rictus said. "Well, let me tell you, she's very happy down there. They all are."

"No they're not!" Harvey raged. "The lake's foul and you know it." He took a step toward Rictus, who retreated as if in fear of his life, which perhaps he was. "How would you like it?" Harvey said, stabbing his finger in Rictus's direction. "Living in the cold and the dark?"

"You're right," said Rictus, raising his hands in surrender. "Whatever you say."

"I say set them *free* now!" Harvey replied. "And if you won't, then *I* will!"

He pushed Rictus aside and started down the stairs two at a time. He didn't have a clue what he was going to do when he got down to the lake—fish were fish, after all, even if they'd once been children; if he tried to take them out of the lake they'd surely drown in the air—but he was determined to somehow save them from Hood.

Rictus came after him down the flight, chattering like a clockwork salesman.

"What do you want?" he said. "Just imagine it and it's yours! How about your own motorcycle?" As he spoke something gleamed on the landing below, and the sleekest motorcycle human eyes had ever seen rolled into view. "It's yours, m'boy!" Rictus said.

"No thanks," Harvey said.

"I don't blame you!" Rictus said, kicking the motorcycle over as he sailed past it. "How about *books?* Do you like books?"

Before Harvey could reply the wall in front of him lifted like a great brick curtain, revealing shelf upon shelf of leather-bound volumes.

"The masterpieces of the world!" Rictus said. "From Aristotle to Zola! No?"

"No!" said Harvey, hurrying on.

"There's got to be *something* you want," Rictus said.

They were heading toward the final flight of stairs now, and Rictus knew he didn't have very long before his prey was out in the open air.

"You like dogs?" Rictus said, as a litter of yapping pups scampered up the stairs. "Pick one! Hell, have 'em all!"

Harvey was tempted, but he stepped over them and on.

"Something more exotic, maybe?" Rictus said, as a flock of brilliantly feathered parrots descended from the ceiling. Harvey waved them away.

"Too noisy, huh?" said Rictus. "You want something quiet and powerful. Tigers! That's what you want! Tigers!"

No sooner said than they padded into view in the hallway below; two white tigers, with eyes like polished gold.

"Nowhere to keep 'em!" Harvey said.

"That's practical!" Rictus conceded. "I like a practical kid."

As the tigers bounded off, the telephone on the table beside the kitchen door began to ring. Rictus was down the flight in two springs, and at the table in another two.

"Listen to this!" he said. "It's the President. He wants to give you a medal!"

"No he doesn't," Harvey said, tiring of this rigamarole now. He was at the bottom of the stairs and crossing to the front door.

"You're right," said Rictus, ear to the phone again. "He wants to give you an oil field, in Alaska!" Harvey kept walking. "No, no, I got that wrong! He wants to give you Alaska!"

"Too cold."

"He says: How about Florida?"

"Too hot."

"Boy! You're a difficult guy to please, Harvey Swick!"

Harvey ignored him, and turned the handle of the front door. Rictus slammed down the phone and raced toward him.

"Wait up!" he hollered, "wait up! I'm not done yet."

"You've got nothing I want," Harvey said, hauling open the front door. "They're all *fakes*."

"What if they are?" said Rictus, suddenly hushed. "So's the sun out there. You can still enjoy it. And let me tell you, it takes a lot of magic to conjure up all these shams and hoaxes. Mr. Hood's really sweating to find you something you like."

Ignoring him, Harvey stepped out onto the porch. Mrs. Griffin was standing on the lawn, with Stew-Cat in her arms, squinting up at the House. She smiled when she saw Harvey emerge.

"I heard such noises," she said. "What's been going on in there?"

"I'll tell you later," said Harvey. "Where's Wendell?"

"He wandered off," she said.

Harvey cupped his hands around his mouth, and yelled: *"Wendell! Wendell!"*

His voice came back to him from the face of the House. But there was no reply from Wendell.

"It's a warm afternoon," said Rictus, idling on the porch. "Maybe he went . . . *swimming.*"

"Oh no," Harvey murmured. "No. Not Wendell. Please, not Wendell . . ."

Rictus shrugged. "He was a goofy little kid, anyhow," he said. "He'll probably look better as a *fish!*"

"No!" Harvey yelled up at the House. "This isn't fair! You can't do this! *You can't!*"

Tears started to cloud his eyes. He wiped them away with his fists. They were both useless, fists and tears. He couldn't soften Hood's heart with weeping, and he couldn't bring down the House with blows. He had no weapon against the enemy but his wits, and his wits were about at an end.

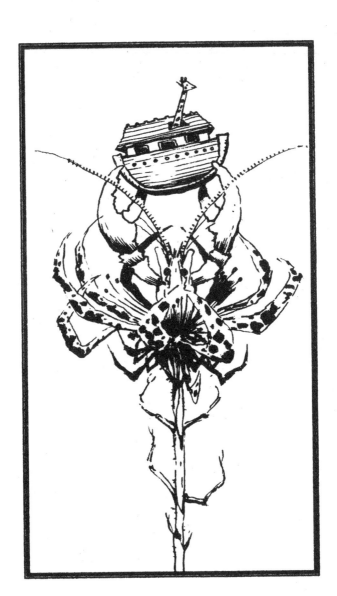

XXII

Appetite

$O_{H, \, TO \, BE \, A \, VAMPIRE \, AGAIN,}$ HARVEY THOUGHT. TO have claws and fangs and a hunger for blood upon him, like the hunger he'd had that distant Halloween; the hunger he'd turned from in disgust. He wouldn't turn from it now. Oh no. He'd let it swell the beast in him, so he could fly in Hood's face with his hatred razor-sharp.

But he wasn't a beast, he was a boy. It was the Vampire King who had the power, not him.

And then, as he stared up at the House, he remembered something that Rictus had told him at the door: "It takes a lot of magic to conjure up these shams and hoaxes," he'd said. "Mr. Hood's really sweating to find you something you like."

Maybe I don't need fangs to suck him dry, Harvey thought; *maybe all I need is wishes.*

"I want to talk to Hood," he told Rictus.

"Why?"

"Well . . . maybe there *are* some things I'd like. Only I want to tell him about them personally."

"He's listening," Rictus said, glancing back toward the House.

Harvey scanned the windows, and the eaves, and the porch, but there was no sign of any presence. "I don't see him," he said.

"Yes you do," Rictus replied.

"Is he in the House?" Harvey asked, staring through the open door.

"Haven't you guessed yet?" Rictus replied. "He *is* the House."

As he spoke a cloud moved over the sun. The roof and walls darkened, and the entire House seemed to swell like a monstrous fungus. It was alive! From the eaves to the foundations, *alive!*

"Go on!" Rictus said. "Speak to him. He's listening."

Harvey took a step toward the House. "Can you hear me?" he said.

The front door swung a little wider, and a sighing breath from the top of the stairs blew a cloud of Jive's dust out onto the porch.

"He can hear you," said Rictus.

"If I stay—" Harvey began.

"Yesss . . . ?" said the House, making the word from creaks and rattles.

"—you'll give me anything I want?"

"For a bright boy like you . . ." came the reply, *". . . anything."*

"You promise? On your magic?"

"I promise. I promise. Just say the word . . ."

"Well, for a start—"

"Yesss?"

"I lost my ark."

"Then you must have another, my lodestar," the Hood-House said. *"Bigger. Better."* And a board of the porch folded back as an ark three times the size of the first one rose into view.

"I don't want *lead* animals," Harvey said as he walked toward the steps.

"What then?" said Hood. *"Silver? Gold?"*

"Flesh and blood," Harvey replied. "Perfect little animals."

"I like a challenge," Hood said, and as he spoke a tinny din of bellows and roars rose from the ark, and the little windows were flung open and the doors flung wide and half a hundred animals appeared, all perfect miniatures: elephants, giraffes, hyenas, aardvarks, doves—

"Satisfied?" said Hood.

Harvey shrugged. "It's okay, I suppose," he said.

"Okay?" said Hood. *"It's a little miracle."*

"So make me another."

"Another ark?"

"Another miracle!"

"What would you like?"

Harvey turned his back on the Hood-House and surveyed the lawn. The sight of Mrs. Griffin, watching with puzzlement, inspired the next request. "I want flowers," he said. *"Everywhere!* And I don't want two alike."

"What for?" asked the Hood-House.

"You said I could have whatever I wanted," Harvey replied. "You didn't say I had to give you reasons. If I have to do that all the fun goes out of it."

"Oh, I wouldn't want that," the Hood-House said. *"You must have fun, at all costs."*

"So give me the flowers," Harvey insisted.

The lawn began to tremble as though a minor earthquake were underway, and the next moment countless shoots pressed up between the blades of grass. Mrs. Griffin began to laugh with delight.

"Look at them!" she said. "Just look!"

It was quite a show; tens of thousands of flowers bursting into blossom at the same time. Harvey could have named a few of them if he'd been quizzed: tulips, daffodils, roses. But most of them were new to him: species that only bloomed at night on the High Himalayas, or on the windswept plateaus of Tierra del Fuego; flowers with blooms as big as his head, or as small as his thumbnail; blooms that stank like bad meat, or smelled like a breeze from Heaven itself.

Even though he knew it was all an illusion, he was impressed, and said so.

"Looks good," he told the Hood-House.

"Satisfied?" it wanted to know.

Was its voice a little weaker than it had been earlier? Harvey wondered. He suspected it was. He showed no sign of that suspicion, however. He simply said: "We're getting there . . ."

"Getting where?" said the Hood-House.

"Well," said Harvey, "I guess we'll know when we arrive."

A low growl of irritation came from the House, shaking the windows. One or two slates slid from the roof and smashed on the ground below.

I'm going to have to be careful, Harvey thought; Hood's getting angry. Rictus echoed that thought.

"I hope you're not stringing Mr. Hood along," he warned, "because he doesn't like that kind of game."

"He wants me happy, doesn't he?" Harvey said.

"Of course."

"So how about something to eat?"

"The kitchen's full," said Rictus.

"I don't want pies and hot dogs. I want—" He paused, ransacking his memory for delicacies he'd heard about. "Roast swan and oysters and those little black eggs—"

"Caviar?" Rictus suggested.

"That's it! I want caviar!"

"Really? It's disgusting."

"I still want it!" said Harvey. "And frog's legs and horse-radish and pomegranates—"

The meals were already appearing in the hallway, plate

upon steaming plate. The smells were tantalizing at first, but the more dishes Harvey added to the list the more sickly the mix became. He rapidly began to exhaust his menu of real meals, however, so instead of giving the House easy recipes like meatballs and pizzas, he started to invent dishes.

"I want crawfish cooked in cherry soda and horse steaks with jelly-bean sauce, and Boston Cream Cheese and pastrami soup—"

"Wait! Wait!" said Rictus. "You're going too fast."

But Harvey didn't stop.

"—and pumpernickel stew and snail fudge with pig's-foot clusters—"

"Wait!" the House howled.

This time, Harvey stopped.

In the heat of his invention he hadn't even looked to see if Hood was supplying him with these eatables, but now he saw all the dishes he'd demanded piled so high in the hallway that they were threatening to topple and float the ark on a noxious sea of sweetmeats and stews.

"I know what you're doing," said the Hood-House.

Uh-oh, Harvey thought; he's onto me.

He looked up from the feast at the door to the façade and saw that his plan to drain the House of its magic was indeed working. Many of the windows were now cracked or broken; the doors were peeling and hanging from their hinges; the porch boards were twisted and blighted.

"You're testing me, aren't you?" said Hood. His voice had never been melodious, but it was now uglier than ever: like the rumble of the Devil's belly. *"Admit it, thief!"* he said.

Harvey took a deep breath, then said: "If I'm going to be your apprentice, I need to know how powerful you are."

"Are you satisfied?" the decaying House demanded.

"Almost," Harvey said.

"What more do you want?" it roared.

What more indeed, Harvey thought. His mind was reeling with these ridiculous lists; he had little left in the way of demands.

"You may have one final gift," the Hood-House said, *"one final proof of my power. Then you must accept me as your Master forever and ever. Agreed?"*

Harvey felt a trickle of cold sweat run down his spine. He stared at the teetering House, his mind racing. What was left to demand?

"Agreed?" the House boomed.

"Agreed," he said.

"So tell me," it went on. *"What do you want?"*

He looked at the tiny animals around the ark, and at the flowers, and at the food spewing through the door. What should he demand? One final request, to break Hood's back. But what? *What?*

A gust of chilly wind came from the direction of the lake. Autumn could not be far off. The season of dying things.

"I know!" he said suddenly.

"Tell me," the House replied, *"tell me and let's have this game over once and for all. I want your bright soul under my wing, little thief."*

"And *I* want the seasons," Harvey said. "All the seasons at once."

"At once?"

"Yes, at once!"

"That's nonsensical!"

"It's what I want."

"Stupid! Imbecilic!"

"It's what I want! You said one more wish and that's it!"

"Very well," said the House. *"I will give it to you. And when you have it, little thief, your soul is mine!"*

XXIII

The War of Seasons

Hood DIDN'T WASTE ANY TIME. HE'D NO SOONER made his final offer to Harvey than the balmy wind grew gusty, carrying off the lamb's wool clouds that had been drifting through the summer sky. In their place came a juggernaut: a thunderhead the size of a mountain, which loomed over the House like a shadow thrown against Heaven.

It had more than lightning at its dark heart. It had the light rains that came at early morning to coax forth the seeds of another spring; it had the drooping fogs of autumn, and the spiraling snows that had brought so many midnight Christmases to the House. Now all three fell at once—rains, snows and fogs—as a chilly sleet that all but covered the sun. It would have killed the flowers on the slope with cold, had the wind not reached them first, tearing through the blossoms with such vehemence that every petal and leaf was snatched up into the air.

Standing between this fragrant tide and the plummeting curtain of ice and cloud, Harvey was barely able to stay upright. But he planted his feet wide apart, and resisted every blast and buffet, determined not to take shelter. This spectacle might be the last he set eyes upon as a free spirit; indeed as a *living* spirit. He intended to enjoy it.

It was a sight to behold; a battle the likes of which the planet had never seen.

To his left, shafts of sunlight pierced the storm clouds in the name of Summer, only to be smothered by Autumn's fogs, while to his right Spring coaxed its legions out of bough and earth, then saw its buds murdered by Winter's frosts before they could show their colors.

Attack after attack was mounted and repulsed, reveille and retreat sounded a hundred times, but no one season was able to carry the day. It was soon impossible to distinguish defeats from victories. The rallies and the feints, the diversions and encirclements all became one confusion. Snows melted into rains as they fell; rains were boiled into vapor, and sweated new shoots out through the rot of their brothers.

And somewhere in the midst of this chaos, the power that had brought it about raised its voice in a rage, demanding that it cease.

"Enough!" the Hood-House yelled. *"Enough!"*

But its voice—which had once carried such terrible authority—had grown weak. Its orders went unnoticed; or if noticed, then disobeyed.

The seasons raged on, throwing themselves against each other with rare abandon, and in passing tearing at the House which stood in the midst of their battlefield.

The walls, which had begun to teeter as Hood's power diminished, were thrown over by the raging wind. The chimneys were wracked by thunder, and toppled; the lightning rods struck so many times they melted, and fell through the slateless roof in a burning rain, setting fire to every floorboard, banister and stick of furniture they touched. The porch, pummeled by hail, was reduced to matchwood. The staircase, rocked to its foundations by the growth in the dirt around it, collapsed like a tower of cards.

Squinting against the face of the storm, Harvey witnessed all of this, and rejoiced. He'd come to the House hoping to steal back the years that Hood had tricked from him, but he'd never dared believe he could bring the whole edifice down. Yet here it was, falling as he watched. Loud though the dins of wind and thunder were, they couldn't drown out the sound of the House as it perished and went to dust. Every nail and sill and brick seemed to shriek at once, a cry of pain that only oblivion could comfort.

Harvey was denied a glimpse of Hood's last moments. A cloud of dirt rose like a veil to cover the sight. But he knew the moment his battle with the Vampire King was over, because the warring seasons suddenly turned to peace. The thunderhead softened its furies, and dispersed; the wind dropped to an idling breeze; the fierce sun grew watery, and veiled itself in mist.

There was debris in the air, of course: petals and leaves, dust and ash. They fell like a dream rain, though their fall marked the end of a dream.

"Oh, child . . ." said Mrs. Griffin.

Harvey turned to her. She was standing just a few yards from him, gazing up at the sky. There was a little patch of blue above their heads; the first glimpse of real sky these few acres of ground had seen since Hood had founded his empire of illusions. But it was not the patch she was watching, it was a congregation of floating lights—the same that Harvey had seen Hood feeding upon in the attic—which had been freed by the collapse of the House. They were now moving in a steady stream toward the lake.

"The children's souls," she said, her voice growing thinner as she spoke the word. "Beautiful."

Her body was no longer solid, Harvey saw; she was fading away in front of him.

"Oh no," he murmured.

She took her eyes off the sky and stared down at her arms, and the cat she was carrying in them. It too was growing insubstantial.

"Look at us," Mrs. Griffin said, with a smile upon her weary face. "It feels so wonderful."

"But you're disappearing."

"I've lingered here far too long, sweet boy," she said. There were tears glistening on her face, but they were tears of joy, not of sadness. "It's time to go . . ." She kept stroking Stew-Cat as they both faded from sight. "You *are* the brightest soul I ever met, Harvey Swick," she said. "Keep shining, won't you?"

Harvey wished he had some words to persuade her to stay a little while longer. But even if he'd had such words, he knew it would have been selfish to speak them. Mrs. Griffin had another life to go to, where every soul shone.

"Good-bye, child," she said. "Wherever I go, I will speak of you with love."

Then her ghostly form flickered out, leaving Harvey alone in the ruins.

XXIV

A Fledgling Thief

HE WAS NOT ALONE FOR LONG. MRS. GRIFFIN AND
Stew-Cat had no sooner vanished from sight than Harvey
heard a voice calling his name. The air was still thick with dust,
and he had to look hard for the speaker. But after a little time
he found her, stumbling toward him.

"Lulu?"

"Who else?" she said, with a little laugh.

The lake's dark water still soaked her from head to foot,
but as it ran from her body and into the ground the last traces
of her silver scales went with it. When she opened her arms to
him, they were human arms.

"You're free!" he said, running to her and hugging her
hard. "I can't believe you're free!"

"We're *all* free," she said, and glanced back toward the
lake.

An extraordinary sight met his eyes: a procession of laughing
children coming toward him through the mist. Those closest
to him were all but returned to their human shape, those
behind them still shaking off their fishiness, step by step.

"We should all get out of here," Harvey said, looking toward the wall. "I don't think we'll have any trouble getting
through the mist now."

One of the children behind Lulu had spotted a box of
clothes in the rubble of the House, and announcing his find
to the rest, stumbled through the debris to find something to
wear. Lulu left Harvey's side to join the search, but not before
she'd planted a kiss on his cheek.

"Don't expect one from me!" said a voice out of the dust,

and Wendell stepped into view, beaming from ear to ear. "What did you do, Harvey?" he wanted to know as he surveyed the chaos. "Pull the place down brick by brick?"

"Something like that," said Harvey, unable to conceal his pride.

There was a roaring sound from the direction of the lake.

"What's that?" Harvey wanted to know.

"The water's disappearing," Wendell said.

"Where to?"

Wendell shrugged. "Who cares?" he said. "Maybe it's all being sucked to Hell!"

Eager to witness this, Harvey walked toward the lake, and through the clouds of dirt in the air saw that it had indeed become a whirlpool, its once placid waters now a raging spiral.

"What happened to Hood, by the way?" Wendell wanted to know.

"He's gone," said Harvey, almost mesmerized by the sight of the vortex. "They've all gone."

Even as the words left his lips a voice said: "Not quite."

He turned from the waters, and there in the rubble stood Rictus. His fine jacket was torn and his face was white with dust. He looked like a clown; a laughing clown.

"Now why would I take myself off?" he asked. "We never said good-bye."

Harvey stared at him with bafflement on his face. Hood was gone; so was his magic. How could Rictus have survived the disappearance of his Master?

"I know what you're thinking," said Rictus, reaching into his pocket. "You're wondering why I'm not dead and gone. Well, I'll tell you. I did some plannin' ahead." He drew a glass globe, which flickered as though it held a dozen candle flames, out of his pocket. "I stole a little piece of the old man's magic, just in case he ever got tired of me and tried to put me out of my misery." He lifted the globe up to his leering face. "I've got enough power here to keep me going for years and years," he said. "Long enough to build a new House, and take over where Hood left off. Oh, don't look so unhappy, kid. I got a place for you, right here—" He slapped his thigh. "You can be my bird dog. I'll send you out lookin' for kiddie-winkies to bring home to Uncle Rictus." He slapped his thigh a second time. "C'mon!" he said. "Don't waste my time now. I don't—"

He stopped there, his gaze dropping to the rubble at his feet.

A terrified whisper escaped his throat. "Oh no . . ." he murmured. "I beg—"

Before he could finish his plea a hand with footlong fingers reached up from the rubble and snatched hold of his throat, dragging him down into the dirt in one swift motion.

"Mine!" said a voice out of the ground. *"Mine!"*

It was Hood, Harvey knew. There was no other voice on earth that cut so deep.

Rictus struggled in his creator's grip, digging in the debris for some weapon. But none came to hand. All he had was his skill as a persuader.

"The magic's yours," he said. "I was holding on to it for you!"

"Liar!" said the voice that rose from the debris.

"I was! I swear!"

"Give it to me then!" Hood demanded.

"Where shall I put it?" Rictus asked, his voice a strangled croak.

Hood's hand loosened him a little, and he managed to haul himself to his knees.

"Right here . . ." Hood said, hanging on to Rictus's collar by his littlest digit, while his forefinger pointed down toward the rubble. *". . . Pour it into the ground."*

"But—"

"Into the ground!"

Rictus pressed the globe between his palms, and it shattered like a sphere of spun sugar, its bright contents running out between his palms and into the ground in front of him.

There was a moment of silence; then a tremor ran through the rubble.

Hood's finger let its captive slip, and Rictus hurriedly got to his feet. He had no chance to make an escape, however. Pieces of timber and stone instantly moved over the heaps of rubble toward the spot where he'd poured the magic, several lifted high into the air. All Rictus could do was cover his head as the hail increased.

Harvey was clear of this flying debris, and might well have made a retreat in these few moments. But he was wiser than that. If he fled now, he knew, his business with Hood would never be finished. It would be like a nightmare he could never quite shake from his head. Whatever happened next, however terrible, it would be better to see it and understand it than to turn his back and have his mind haunt him with imaginings to his dying day.

He didn't have to wait long for Hood's next move. The hand holding Rictus's neck suddenly let him go, and in a flash was gone from sight. The following moment the ground gaped and a form appeared, hunched over as it climbed out of its tomb in the rubble.

Rictus let out a cry of horror, but it was short. Before he could retreat one step the figure reached for him, and turning to face Harvey, held his traitorous servant high.

Here, at last, was the evil that had built the Holiday House, shaped more or less as a man. He was not made of flesh, blood and bone, however. He had used the magic Rictus had unwillingly provided to create another body.

In the high times of his evil, Hood had been the House. Now, it was the other way around. The House, what was left of it, had become Mr. Hood.

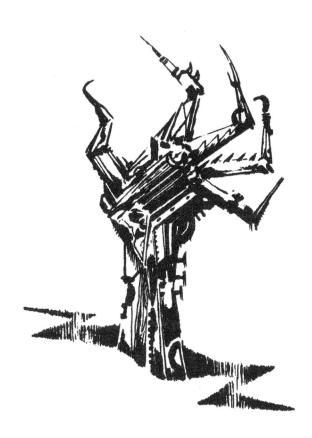

XXV

The Vortex

His eyes were made of broken mirrors, and his face of gouged stone. He had a mane of splinters, and limbs of timber. He had shattered slates for teeth, and rusty screws for fingernails, and a cloak of rotted drapes that scarcely hid the darkness of his heart from sight.

"*So, thief—*" he said, ignoring Rictus's pitiful struggles, "*—you see me as the man I was. Or rather, as a copy of that man. Is it what you expected?*"

"Yes," Harvey said. "It's exactly what I expected."

"*Oh?*"

"You're dirt and muck and bits and pieces," Harvey said. "You're nothing!"

"*Nothing, am I?*" said Hood. "*Nothing? Ha! I'll show you, thief! I'll show you what I am.*"

"Let me kill him for you," Rictus managed to gasp. "You needn't bother! I'll do it!"

"*You brought him here,*" Hood said, turning his splintered eyes on his servant. "*You're to blame!*"

"He's just a boy. I can deal with him. Just let me do it! Let me—"

Before Rictus could finish Hood took hold of his servant's head, and with one short motion simply twisted it off. A yellowish cloud of foul-smelling air rose from the severed neck, and Rictus—the last of Hood's abominable quartet—perished in an instant. Hood let the head go from his hand. It flew up into the air like an unknotted balloon, giving off a farting sputter as it looped the loop and finally fell, emptied, to the ground.

Hood casually dropped the body, which had summarily shrunk to nothing, and turned his mirrored gaze back upon Harvey.

"Now, thief," he said. *"YOU WILL SEE POWER!"*

His mane of splinters stood on end, as though every one of them was ready to pierce Harvey's heart. His mouth grew wide as a tunnel, and a blast of sour, icy air rose from his belly.

"Come closer," he roared, opening his arms.

The rags that clung there billowed, and spread like the wings of some ancient vampire; a vampire that had dined on the blood of pterodactyl and tyrannosaur.

"Come!" he said again. *"Or must I come for you?"*

Harvey didn't waste his breath with a reply. He'd need every gasp he had if he was to outpace this horror. Not even certain what direction he was taking, he turned on his heels and ran, as another blast of soul-freezing air struck him. The ground was treacherous; slippery and strewn with rubble. He fell within six strides, and glanced back to see Hood descending upon him with a vengeful shriek. He hauled himself to his feet—Hood's rusted nails missing him by a whistling inch—and had taken three stumbling strides from Hood's shadow when he heard Lulu calling his name.

He veered in the direction of her voice, but Hood caught the collar of his jacket.

"Got you, little thief!" he roared, dragging Harvey back into his splintery embrace.

Before Hood could catch better hold, however, Harvey threw back his arms and pitched himself forward. Off came the jacket, and he made a third dash for freedom, his eyes fixed on Lulu, who was beckoning him toward her.

She was standing on the edge of the lake, he realized, perched inches from the spinning waters. Surely she didn't imagine they could escape into the lake? The vortex would tear them limb from limb.

"We can't—" he yelled to Lulu.

"We *must!*" she called back. "It's the only way!"

He was within three strides of her now. He could see her bare feet slithering and sliding on the slimy rock as she fought to keep her balance. He reached out for her, determined to snatch her from her perch before she fell, but her eyes weren't on him. They were on the monster at his back.

"Lulu!" he yelled to her. "Don't look!"

But her gaze was fixed upon Hood, her mouth agape, and Harvey couldn't help but glance back to see what fascinated her so.

Hood's pursuit had thrown his coat of rags into disarray, and there was something between its folds, he saw, darker than any night sky or lightless cellar. What was it? The essence of his magic, perhaps, guarding his loveless heart?

"Do you give up?" Hood said, driving Harvey back onto the rocks beside Lulu. *"Surely you would not choose the vortex over me?"*

"Go . . ." Harvey murmured to Lulu, his gaze still fixed on the mystery beneath Hood's coat.

He felt her hand grasp his for a moment. "It's the only way," she said. Then her fingers were gone, and he was standing on the rocks alone.

"If you choose the flood you will die horribly," Hood was saying. *"It will spin you apart. Whereas I—"* He extended an inviting hand to Harvey, stepping up onto the rock as he did so. *"—I offer you an easy death, rocked to sleep on a bed of illusions."* He made a smile, and it was the foulest sight Harvey had ever seen. *"Choose,"* he said.

Out of the corner of his eye Harvey glimpsed Lulu. She had not fled, as he'd thought; she'd simply gone to find a weapon. And she had one: a piece of timber dragged out of the rubble. It would be precious little use against Hood's enormity, Harvey knew, but he was glad not to be alone in these last moments.

He looked up at Hood's face.

"Maybe I *should* sleep—" he said.

The Vampire King smiled. *"Wise little thief,"* he replied, opening his arms to invite the boy into his shadow.

Harvey took a step over the rock toward Hood, raising his hand as he did so. His face was reflected in the shattered mirrors of the vampire's eyes: two thieves in one head.

"Sleep," said Hood.

But Harvey had no intention of sleeping yet. Before Hood could stop him, he grabbed hold of the creature's coat and pulled. The scraps came away with a wet tearing sound, and Hood let out a howl of rage as he was uncovered.

There was no great enchantment at his heart. In fact, there was no heart at all. There was only a void—neither cold nor hot, living nor dead—made not of mystery but of nothingness. The illusionist's illusion.

Furious at this revelation, Hood let out another roar of rage, and reached down to reclaim the rags of his coat from the thief's hands. Harvey took a quick step backward, however, avoiding the fingers by a whisker. Hood came raging after him, his soles squealing on the rock, leaving Harvey with no choice but to retreat another step, until he had nowhere to go but the flood.

Again, Hood snatched at the filched rags, and would have had both coat and thief in one fatal grasp had Lulu not run at him from behind, swinging the timber like a baseball bat. She struck the back of Hood's knee so hard her weapon shattered, the impact pitching her to the ground.

The blow was not without effect, however. It threw Hood off balance, and he flailed wildly, the thunder of the vortex shaking the rock on which he and Harvey perched and threatening to toss them both into the maelstrom. Even now, Hood was determined to claim his rags back from Harvey, and conceal the void in him.

"Give me my coat, thief!" he howled.

"It's all yours!" Harvey yelled, and tossed the stolen rags toward the waters.

Hood lunged after them, and as he did so Harvey flung himself back toward solid ground. He heard Hood shriek behind him, and turned to see the Vampire King—the rags in his fist—pitch headfirst into the frenzied waters.

The maned head surfaced a moment later, and Hood struck out for the bank, but strong as he was the vortex was stronger. It swept him away from the rocks, drawing him toward its center, where the waters were spiraling down into the earth.

In terror, he started to plead for assistance, his pitiful bargains only audible when the whirlpool carried him to the bank where Harvey and Lulu now stood.

"Thief!" he yelled. *"Help me, and . . . I'll give you . . . the world! For . . . ever . . . and ever . . ."*

Then the ferocity of the waters began to rip at his make-shift body, tearing out his nails and rattling out his teeth, washing away his mane of splinters, and shaking his limbs apart at the joints. Reduced to a living litter of flotsam and jetsam, he was drawn into the white waters at the whirlpool's heart, and shrieking with rage, went where all evil must go at last: into nothingness.

On the shore Harvey put his arms around Lulu, laughing and sobbing at the same time.

"We did it . . ." he said.

"Did what?" said a voice at their backs, and they looked around to see Wendell wandering toward them, blithe as ever. Every article of clothing he'd found in the rubble was either too large or too small.

"What's been going on?" he wanted to know. "What are you laughing at? What are you crying for?" He looked beyond Harvey and Lulu, in time to see the last fragments of Hood's body disappear with a fading howl. "And what was *that?*" he demanded.

Harvey wiped the tears from his cheeks, and got to his feet. At last, he had a purpose for Wendell's perpetual reply.

"Who cares?" he said.

XXVI

Living Proof

THE WALL OF MIST STILL HOVERED AT THE EDGE OF Hood's domain, and it was there that the survivors gathered to say their farewells. None quite knew what adventures lay on the other side of the mist, of course. Each of the children had come into the House from a different year. Would they all find that age—give or take a month or two—awaiting them on the other side?

"Even if we don't get the stolen years back," Lulu said as they prepared to step into the mist, "we're free because of you, Harvey."

There were murmurs of thanks from the little crowd, and a few grateful tears.

"Say something," Wendell hissed to Harvey.

"Why?"

"Because you're a hero."

"I don't feel like one."

"So tell them that."

Harvey raised his hands to hush the murmurs. "I just want to say . . . we'll probably all forget about being here in a little while . . ." A few of the children said: *no we won't;* or, *we'll always remember you.* But Harvey insisted: "We will," he said. "We'll grow up and we'll forget. Unless . . ."

"Unless what?" asked Lulu.

"Unless we remind ourselves every morning. Or make a story of it, and tell everyone we meet."

"They won't believe us," said one of the children.

"That doesn't matter," said Harvey. "*We'll* know it's true, and that's what counts."

This met with approval from all sides.

"Now let's go home," said Harvey. "We've wasted too much time here already."

Wendell nudged him in the ribs as the group dispersed. "What about telling them you're not a hero?" he said.

"Oh, yeah," said Harvey with a mischievous smile. "I forgot about that."

The first of the children were already braving the wall of mist, eager to put the horrors of Hood's prison behind them as soon as possible. Harvey watched them fading with every step they took, and wished he'd had a moment to talk to them; to find out who they were and why they'd wandered into Hood's grip. Had they been orphans, with no other place to call home; or runaways, like Wendell and Lulu; or simply bored with their lives, the way he'd been bored, and seduced by illusions?

He would never know. They were disappearing one by one, until there was only Lulu, Wendell and himself left on the inside of the wall.

"Well," Wendell said to Harvey, "if time really *is* set to rights out there, then I'm going back a few more years than you."

"That's true."

"If we meet again, I'm going to be a lot older. You may not even know me."

"I'll know you," Harvey said.

"Promise?" said Wendell.

"I promise."

With that they shook hands, and Wendell made his departure into the mist. He was gone in three strides.

Lulu sighed heavily. "Have you ever wanted two things at the same time," she asked Harvey, "but you knew you couldn't have both of them?"

"Once or twice," said Harvey. "Why?"

"Because I'd like to grow up with you, and be your friend,"

she replied, "but I also want to go home. And I think in the year that's waiting for me on the other side of that wall, you haven't even been born."

Harvey nodded sadly, glancing back toward the ruins. "I guess we do have *one* thing to thank Hood for."

"What's that?"

"We were children together," he said, taking hold of her hand. "At least for a little while."

Lulu tried to smile, but her eyes were full of tears.

"Let's go together as far as we can," Harvey said.

"Yes, I'd like that," Lulu replied, and hand in hand they walked toward the wall. At the last moment before the mist eclipsed them they looked around at each other, and Harvey said: "Home . . ."

Then they stepped into the wall. For the first stride he felt Lulu's hand in his, but by the second stride it had grown faint, and by the third—when he stepped out into the street—it and she had gone completely, delivered back into the time from which she'd stepped, all those seasons ago.

Harvey looked up at the sky. The sun had set, but its pinkish light still found the ribs of cloud laid high above him. The wind was gusty, and chilled the sweat of fear and exertion on his face and spine.

Teeth chattering, he started home through the darkening streets, uncertain what awaited him.

IT WAS STRANGE THAT AFTER SO MANY VICTORIES THE simple business of walking home should defeat him, but defeat him it did. After an hour of wandering, his wits and strength—which had preserved him from every terror Hood could conjure—failed him. His head began to spin, his legs buckled beneath him, and he fell down on the sidewalk, exhausted.

Luckily two passersby took pity on him, and gently asked

him where he lived. It was dangerous, he vaguely recalled, to trust his life to total strangers, but he had no choice. All he could do was give himself over to their care, and hope that the world he'd returned to still had a little kindness in it.

HE WOKE IN DARKNESS, AND FOR ONE HEARTSTOPPING moment he thought the black lake had claimed him after all, and he was down in its depths, a prisoner.

Crying out in terror he sat up, and to his infinite relief saw the window at the bottom of his bed, the curtains slightly parted, and heard the light patter of rain upon the sill. He was home.

He swung his legs out of bed and stood up. His whole body ached as though he'd gone ten rounds with a heavyweight boxer, but he was strong enough to hobble to the door and open it.

The sound of two familiar voices drifted up from the bottom of the stairs.

"I'm just happy he's home," he heard his mom say.

"So am I," said his dad. "But we need some explanations."

"We'll get them," his mom went on. "But we shouldn't push him too hard."

Clinging to the banisters as he went, Harvey started down the stairs, while his mom and dad continued to talk.

"We need to find out the truth quickly," his father said. "I mean, suppose he was involved with something criminal?"

"Not Harvey."

"Yes, Harvey. You saw the state of him. Blood and dirt all over him. He's not been out picking roses, that's for sure."

At the bottom of the stairs Harvey halted, a little afraid to face the truth. Had anything changed, or were the two people just out of sight still old and frail?

He went to the door and pushed it open. His mom and

dad were standing with their backs to him at the window, staring out at the rain.

"Hello," he said.

They both turned at the same moment, and Harvey let out a whoop of joy to see that all the griefs and horrors of the House had not been endured in vain. Here was his prize, staring down at him: his mother and father, looking just the way they had before Rictus had come for him. The stolen years were back where they belonged, in *his* possession.

"I'm a good thief," he said, half to himself.

"Oh, my darling," said his mom, coming to him with open arms.

He hugged her first, then his dad.

"What have you been up to, son?" his dad wanted to know.

Harvey remembered how difficult it had been to explain everything last time; so instead of even trying he said: "I was just wandering around and I got lost. I didn't mean to get you upset."

"You said something about a thief."

"Did I?"

"You know you did," his dad said sternly.

"Well . . . are you a thief if you're taking something that belongs to you in the first place?" Harvey asked him.

His dad and mom exchanged puzzled looks.

"No, honey," his mom said. "Of course not."

"Then I'm not a thief," Harvey replied.

"I think you owe both of us the truth, Harvey," his mom said. "We want to know everything."

"Everything?"

"Everything," said his dad.

So he told them the whole tale, just as they'd asked, right from the beginning, and if their expressions had been doubtful the last time he'd related his adventures, they were incredulous now.

"Do you *really* expect us to believe all of this?" his father broke in while Harvey was talking about meeting Hood in the attic.

"I can take you to the House," Harvey said. "Or what's left of it. I couldn't find it last time, because it hid itself from grown-ups. But Hood's gone, so there's no magic left to hide it with."

Once again his mom and dad exchanged baffled looks.

"If you can find this Hood-House," his father said, "we'd both like to see it."

THEY SET OUT EARLY THE FOLLOWING DAY, AND THIS time—just as Harvey had expected—the way back to the House was not concealed by magic. He found the streets that Rictus had first led him along easily enough, and very soon the gentle slope on which the House had once stood came into view.

"That's it," he said to his mom and dad. "The House stood there."

"It's just a hill, Harvey," his dad said. "A hill covered in grass."

It was indeed a surprise to see that the ground on which so many terrible deeds had been done had greened so quickly.

"It all looks rather pretty," his mom said as they came to the place where the mist wall had stood.

"The ruins are under there, I swear," Harvey said, venturing onto the slope. "I'll show you. Come on."

They weren't the only visitors here today. There were several kite-flyers plying the wind at the top of the ridge; a dozen or more dogs romping around; children laughing as they rolled down the slope; even a pair of lovers, whispering in each other's ears.

Harvey resented the presence of all these people. How *dare* they romp and laugh and fly their kites here, he thought, as though it were just another hill? He wanted to tell them all that they were cavorting on the ruins of a *vampire's* house, and see how quickly that wiped the smiles off their faces.

But then, he thought, perhaps it was better this way; better that the hill not be haunted by rumors and stories. The name of Hood would probably never cross the lips of these lovers and kite-flyers, and why should it? His evil had no place in happy hearts.

"Well?" said Harvey's dad as the three of them climbed the slope. "This House of yours is well buried."

Harvey went down on his haunches and dug at the dirt with his bare hands. The ground was soft, and gave off the sweet smell of fertility.

"Strange, isn't it?" said a voice.

He looked up from his labors, both his fists full of dirt. A man a little older than his father was standing a few yards from him, smiling.

"What are you talking about?" Harvey asked.

"The flowers. The ground," he said. "Maybe the earth has its own magic—good magic, I mean—and it's buried Hood's memory forever."

"You know about Hood?" Harvey said.

The man nodded. "Oh yes."

"What exactly *do* you know?" Harvey's mom asked. "Our son here's been telling us such strange stories . . ."

"They're all true," the man said.

"You haven't even heard them," Harvey's dad replied.

"You should trust your boy," the man said. "I have it on the best authority that he's a hero."

Harvey's dad stared at his son with a twitch of a smile on his face. "Really?" he said. "Were you one of Hood's prisoners?"

"Not me," the man said.

"Then how do you know?"

The man glanced over his shoulder, and there at the bottom of the slope stood a woman in a white dress.

Harvey studied this stranger, trying to make out her face, but her wide-brimmed hat kept her features in shadow. He started to get to his feet, intending to take a closer look, but the man said: "Don't . . . *please*. She sent me in her place, just to say hello. She remembers you the way you are—young, that is—and she'd like you to remember her the same way."

"Lulu . . ." Harvey murmured.

The man neither confirmed nor denied this. He simply said to Harvey: "I am much obliged to you, young man. I hope to be as fine a husband to her as you were a friend."

"Husband?" Harvey mouthed.

"How time flies," the man said, consulting his watch. "We're late for lunch. May I shake your hand, young sir?"

"It's dirty," Harvey warned, letting the earth run between the fingers of his right hand.

"What could be better between us," the man replied with a smile, "than this . . . *healing* earth?"

He took Harvey's hand, shook it, and with a nod to Harvey's mom and dad hurried back down the slope.

Harvey watched as he spoke to the woman in the white dress; saw her nod; saw her smile in his direction. Then they were both gone, out into the street and away.

"Well . . ." said Harvey's dad, ". . . it seems your Mr. Hood existed after all."

"So you believe me?" Harvey asked.

"Something happened here," came the reply, "and you were a hero. I believe that."

"Then that's enough," said Harvey's mom. "You don't have to keep digging, sweetie. Whatever's under there should stay buried."

Harvey was about to empty his left hand of dirt when his dad said: "Let me have that," and opened his hand.

"Really?" said Harvey.

"I've heard a little good magic's always useful," came his father's reply. "Isn't that right?"

Harvey smiled, and poured a fistful of earth into his father's palm.

"Always," he said.

THE DAYS THAT FOLLOWED WERE UNLIKE ANY HARVEY had ever known. Though there was no more talk of Hood, or of the House, or of the green hill upon which it had once stood, the subject was a part of every look and laugh that passed between him and his parents.

He knew they had only the vaguest sense of what had happened to them, but they were all three agreed on one thing: that it was fine to be together again.

Time would be precious from now on. It would tick by, of course, as it always had, but Harvey was determined he wouldn't waste it with sighs and complaints. He'd fill every moment with the seasons he'd found in his heart: hopes like birds on a spring branch; happiness like a warm summer sun; magic like the rising mists of autumn. And best of all, love; love enough for a thousand Christmases.

About the Author

CLIVE BARKER IS THE INTERNATIONALLY BESTSELLING author of more than twenty books for adults and children. He is also a widely acclaimed artist, film producer, screenwriter, and director. He lives with his partner, the renowned photographer David Armstrong, in Beverly Hills.

OH, THE HORRORS!

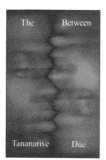

The Between
Tananarive Due

Bird Box
Josh Malerman

Classic Works of Horror
Edgar Allan Poe

Dracula
Bram Stoker

$12 EACH

William Peter Blatty
The Exorcist

Lovecraft Country
Matt Ruff

The Thief of Always
Clive Barker

When the Reckoning Comes
LaTanya McQueen

OLIVE EDITIONS | AVAILABLE FOR A LIMITED TIME ONLY

HARPER ● PERENNIAL